THE RETURN OF THE WITCH

M. J. CAAN

Vinci Books

vinci-books.com

Published by Vinci Books Ltd in 2026

1

Copyright © M.J. Caan 2019

The author has asserted their moral right to be identified as the author of this work in accordance with the Copyright, Designs and Patents Act 1988.
This work is a work of fiction. Names, characters, places and incidents are the product of the author's imagination or are used fictitiously. Any resemblance to actual persons, living or dead, places and incidents is entirely coincidental.
All rights reserved. No part of this publication may be copied, reproduced, distributed, stored in any retrieval system, or transmitted in any form or by any means, including photocopying, recording, or other electronic or mechanical methods, nor used as a source for any form of machine learning including AI datasets, without the prior written permission of the publisher.
The publisher and the author have made every effort to obtain permissions for any third party material used in this book and to comply with copyright law. Any queries in this respect should be brought to the attention of the publisher and any omissions will be corrected in future editions.
A CIP catalogue record for this book is available from the British Library.
Paperback ISBN: 9781036704483
The EU GPSR authorised representative is Logos Europe, 9 rue Nicolas Poussion, 17000 La Rochelle, France contact@logoseurope.eu

By M.J. Caan

The Shifter Wars

The Girl with the Good Magic
Enter the Wolf
The Return of the Witch

Paranormal Fades

Midlife Crashing
Midlife Burning
Midlife Rising

Midlife Enclave

Tantric Hexes
Tantric Bindings

Earth's First

Earth's First
Dark Days
A Hero Rises
Rise Of The Acolytes

Singing Falls Witches

Hex After Forty
That Good Hex
How Torie Got Her Hex Back
Hex and Chocolate
Moonlight Hexes
Hex and the Single Witch
Hex Education
Hex After Dark
That Hex Factor

For Brian. The only Totem I need.

Prologue

AN UNINVITED GUEST FOR DINNER

Admittedly, I was terrified.

It took every ounce of willpower I had not to summon my magic and throw it at the mess in front of me. Honestly, I didn't know what would happen if I did use magic. I had never tried it in a situation like this before. Resisting the urge, I wiped my brow and leaned in closer to look at the soft white peaks that were rising before me.

"Allie, are you sure you want to do this?" It was my Aunt Lena leaning in to whisper in my ear. "You have to be careful. One little mistake and it will be all over."

"You think I don't know that? Now back up, you're too close; you're making me doubt myself."

It was too late to stop now; I was all in.

I found myself holding my breath as I reached forward and turned off the stand mixer sitting on the kitchen counter. I eased the blade up and out of the bowl, marveling at the perfect stiff peaks of egg whites I had beaten. They clung to the blades with just the right consistency, and the soft yet firm waves inside the bowl looked like silky, frosty peaks that had frozen in time just as they crested.

Perfect. Now to get them folded into the orange base sauce I had cooked, and into the ramekins without overmixing them. The thought of ruining this was making me break out in a sweat. Christ, I hadn't felt this kind of pressure when fighting werewolves and vampires. That was a walk in the park compared to making a perfect orange soufflé with a Grand Marnier topping.

"Allie, are you sure about this?" Aunt Lena said, wringing her hands. "I mean, it's not too late to put in a peach pie. I bought a brand new tub of vanilla bean that will be perfect on it."

"No, Aunt Lena. This is my first big meal having Hope over since everything with her parents. It has to be perfect. She loves dessert and I intend to blow her out of the water with this one."

"Well, I'd say the main course certainly did that," Aunt Lena replied.

She was right, of course. For dinner I'd made grilled swordfish with provencal sauce. It was delicious, if I must say so myself. Combined with the grilled asparagus and endive salad with champagne vinaigrette, it had been the best meal I'd ever made, and Hope had been more than just a little impressed. But this would take the evening to a whole new level; this would send her into sensory overdrive.

If I could get it into the oven and it baked perfectly. Without collapsing. I'd die if it collapsed. And I was pretty sure that no magic spell in the world would fix this if I fucked it up. I could probably fix a fallen angel easier than I could a fallen soufflé.

Aunt Lena opened the oven door for me and I gingerly placed the mini ramekins into the lower third, praying they would rise just right, and not have burned tops. Exhaling, I turned to high-five my aunt before setting the timer for thirty minutes. Not that I trusted the timer; I would watch these bad boys like a hawk.

"Shall I offer everyone tea while we wait?" Aunt Lena asked.

"Thanks, but no. I think this calls for something little more special." I went to the large refrigerator and retrieved a bottle of pink Prosecco. "Tonight deserves a bit of bubbly, I think."

Aunt Lena's face lit up and she clapped her hands in glee. "Vivian will not approve, but I think you're right. I'll get the good glasses." She set about collecting six champagne glasses and arranging them on a serving tray, while I removed saucers from the cupboards on which to serve the little soufflé when they came out of the oven.

"What is that I smell?" said Hope, walking into the kitchen.

"Hey! It's a surprise! Go back outside. We'll be out in a few with some drinks before dessert," I said.

"Oh, you know I love me some dessert! What is it?" She attempted to peak into the oven, but a single glance from me caused her to throw her arms up in resignation and head back out onto the deck where we the table was set. I could hear laughter through the open French doors that led outside, and for a moment, I almost forgot the world of shit we were all in.

The tray full of glasses and bottle was a little wobbly in my hands as I made my way outside.

"Here, let me help," said Hope, taking some of the glasses and setting them on the outdoor coffee table that was positioned between a sofa and two chairs at one end of the deck.

"Yes! Champagne!" said my brother Gar, giving a small fist pump.

"No way," I said. I nodded at a second bottle on the tray. "That's for you and Jhamal. Sparkling cider."

He fake grumbled, but reached for the glasses nonetheless. He winked at me knowingly. We both knew it wouldn't be his first sip. I wiped the sweat from my palms on the back of my jeans, hoping no one noticed.

Hosting a dinner party in the midst of a war against a vampire with an army of werewolves and a Warlock at his disposal might not have been my best idea. But I needed to mend things with Hope. She was my best friend, and because of my actions, her parents had been horribly murdered. Okay, maybe it wasn't entirely my fault, but I certainly felt guilty.

No matter how I tried to spin it to myself, I kept thinking: what would have happened if I had never shown up with Cody at her house that first night? The night he shifted and we were attacked by members of the Order of the Fell. Had I never been at Hope's house, she would have never been on the Warlock's radar. And if she hadn't been on their radar, then maybe her parents would still be alive.

And our friendship wouldn't have taken the weird turn it had.

Harsh words had been spoken and feelings had been hurt. But Hope was more than a friend; she was as much a part of my family as my aunts and Gar. So I had visited her while she was in the hospital under evaluation after the death of her parents. We yelled. We cried. And ultimately, we forgave. Or rather, she forgave. Me? I mostly just groveled and offered words and my heart. In the end it was enough to get her talking to me again. But I knew better than anyone that some wounds can fester long after the skin has healed over them.

That was why I had demanded that she stay in the guest bedroom until she was ready to start thinking about what to do with her parents' house. Today was her first day after moving in, so I was determined to make it special. The dinner and the dessert were key comforts we had always bonded over, and the least I could do was make these memorable.

I hadn't invited my boyfriend Cody, and he understood why. While he had the best of intentions towards Hope, and I didn't doubt the love he had for me, he was still a werewolf—and werewolves had killed Hope's parents. No point in poking that bear again.

My aunts were onboard with her staying here, and I know Gar had no issues with it either. After what we had all been through in the last week, we all recognized the importance of family. No more lone wolves; this pack was staying together no matter what was thrown our way.

The bubbly was exactly what I needed. Light, fruity, and just the right amount of buzz-inducing, without being overpowering. Part of me was still focused on listening for the timer to go off, and it was all I could do to resist going back into the kitchen to peek into the oven and seeing what my little ramekins of goodness were doing.

"So Allie," said Gar, "it's been awfully quiet the last week. Do you think Mallis and company have moved on?"

The silence that fell over the deck was deafening. I wanted to frown at my brother, but he was looking at me with such earnestness that I felt my heart breaking. Jhamal placed one hand behind Gar's back and rubbed his shoulder comfortingly; I knew without asking that Gar was afraid for his boyfriend. Jhamal and his aunt had been kidnapped by the Warlock and Mallis to be used as bait—to get to me. By working together, my friends and I had managed to save everyone, but I was sure the thought of what could have happened was still very fresh in Gar's mind.

"This is a war, Gar," I said. "I don't think they just gathered their troops and went home. Something tells me they're biding their time."

"And what about us?" he replied. "I mean, what about you guys? What are you planning to do to stop him?"

"Gar," said Aunt Vivian, "now's not the time to discuss this."

"Well when is?" he replied. "Are we waiting for them to attack again? To kidnap or murder someone else we love?"

I sensed Hope flinch at that one and I gave Gar a look that shut him down.

"I'm sorry," he said, addressing Hope. "I didn't mean that to come out like it did."

"It's okay, Gar," Hope said. "I know what you mean. For what it's worth, Allie, I'd like to know what the next steps are going to be as well. I've seen firsthand what these monsters can do...I don't wish that on anyone. So if you have a plan, we should talk about it."

"The last plan I had nearly got us killed," I said. I slumped down onto the sofa next to Hope and let my head fall lazily onto her shoulder.

"No," said Jhamal, "your plan kept my aunt and me from being killed. I saw the ruthlessness that Warlock has. Do you think he's sitting back on his laurels somewhere waiting for you to make a move? Doubtful. Whatever they were planning, they are moving forward with it. Now."

"I hate to say it, but the kid is right," said Aunt Lena. We all knew she was joking. Out of everyone she had taken an immediate liking to Jhamal and the term "kid" was her way of ribbing him. "The eclipse is less than two weeks away. We still don't know anything about how the Warlock will go about creating this Leveling spell, let alone how to stop it."

I shuddered on the inside at the mention of the spell. The Warlock believed that it was possible, with the right magic, to halt the eclipse, creating a permanent night over the town of Trinity Cove. If he succeeded, his master, the vampire known as Mallis, would have free reign over this town. And since this town was sitting on top of a veritable gold mine of innate magical elements that flowed freely throughout the bedrock, he would be able to unleash a supernatural apocalypse; a new Hell on Earth.

But that wasn't going to happen. Not on my watch, at least. As Reliquary, I was able to store vast amounts of magic and use it at my will. Surely there was a way to stop this madness from happening. But right now, I couldn't think about any of that—the timer in the kitchen had just buzzed, and I jumped up and ran inside.

The smell in the kitchen was divine, and I knew that as soon as I opened the oven door, the aroma would waft outside and set everyone's tastebuds on fire. I carefully picked up the baking sheet with the ramckins arrayed on it. The soufflés were golden, high, and light. Perfect set. I couldn't wait to get them dusted with powdered sugar and covered in orange liqueur topping.

And, as luck would have it, that was when the warning alarms attached to the wards that protected the house went off.

I felt the brush against my skin. It was like someone had just taken a hairbrush out of the freezer and applied it to my scalp. The soufflés deflated like Tom Brady's football when I dropped them on the island.

"Damnit!" I said as I ran out onto the deck. Aunt Lena and Aunt Vivian, the only others in the house that could have felt the warning, were already looking out over the deck railing.

"What is it? What's going on?" asked Hope, moving away from the three of us. Fear played across her features. She had been around the occult long enough to know when something was about to go down.

"Something just set the wards off," said Aunt Vivian, not taking her eyes off the tree line at the back of our property.

We looked out over the backyard, focusing on the wooded area behind the house. It was getting dark, making it hard to see what exactly was out there.

"Hope, take Gar back into the house," I said. I summoned a small bit of magic and held it at the ready. Judging from the buzz in the air, my aunts were doing the same.

Before Hope—or more likely Gar—could protest, I felt it again. Only this time, the hit on the wards was harder and far more deliberate. It'd definitely come from the back perimeter.

"Got it," said Aunt Lena. "I recognize that creatures bio-signature."

"Indeed," replied Aunt Vivian, glancing over at me. "Vampire."

Chapter One

"Stay here and protect Gar and Hope," I said to my aunts. "Jhamal, you're with me."

Jhamal nodded, and in the blink of eye he shifted into his lion form. The deck boards creaked under his weight as he padded over to stand next to me. I wrapped a bunch of his golden mane in my hand as he leapt over the railing. In midair I swung my leg over his back so that when he made contact with the ground I was sitting astride him. Together, we moved down the steep slope of the backyard towards the line of trees.

"Can you see him?" I asked.

Jhamal only nodded his large head as he walked purposefully towards a shadowy figure standing behind a massive pine tree. The thought of approaching a vampire after having gone through what I had only a week earlier caused my magic to flare protectively around us. I reached out with my mind, probing for more signatures that might tell me how many vampires there actually were. But his was the only *ping* I received from my mystical sonar.

Only one vamp. For some reason, that made the bloodsucker even scarier.

"I am alone," came a voice from behind the branches of the tree. Jhamal stopped about twenty feet away, and waited.

"Come out where we can see you," I said. There was some rustling of the branches, but no real movement. "Fine." I cast a ball of magical light into the air above the tree and willed it to luminesce outward. The vampire held up one arm to shield his eyes from the light and stepped forward, away from the shadows.

"I'm not here to hurt anyone," it said. "My name is Elion and I am not here to fight."

He stood away from the trees, stopping mere inches from the invisible ward that snaked around our property. The blue light from my magic illuminated him clearly and allowed me to make out most of his features. He was startlingly pale, with neatly-cropped dark hair atop a thin, angular face dominated by black eyes. Not just the pupils, or even the irises were black—the entire orbital structure was black, with tiny flecks of molten gold that danced in the darkness. He was slender of build, dressed in well-fitting jeans and a long-sleeved, light blue t-shirt. The shirt was stained with dark patches splattered across the chest and down the entire right arm.

Jhamal growled menacingly at the vampire—I didn't need him to tell me that the creature was covered in blood. Throwing one leg over Jhamal's back I slipped down off the great lion and walked over to the vampire. I stopped just before I reached the ward. To my magically-enhanced senses, it looked like a glowing blue wall with sparks of lightning spiderwebbing throughout. I trusted that the vampire would not be able to reach—or more importantly, bite—through.

Sensing Jhamal's discomfort, I waved reassuringly at him. Nonetheless, part of me was pleased to see the tension in the Lion-Shifter's body; he was prepared to attack at the first sign of any aggression from the creature that stood before us. The vampire looked over at Jhamal, taking in his massive form with those emotionless black eyes.

I sent a thread of magic through the ward and wrapped it around the vampire, probing for anything that might be… off. Not that I knew quite what to look for—just the fact that he was a vampire was enough to give me a serious case of the willies. But I figured that maybe my magic would pick up on any weird mystical weapons he might be hiding, or any truly evil intentions. Satisfied, I addressed him in the most non-shaky voice I could muster.

"What are you doing here?"

He took a deep breath, which surprised me. I didn't think vamps breathed, being dead and all.

"I need your… help." His voice was deep, but strained, his wording uneven.

Despite myself, I burst out laughing. "My help? How stupid does your master think I am?"

"I have no master, young witch." What I said must have sparked something in him; his eyes seemed to blaze a little more to life, and a hardness crept into his voice that caused a chill to race up my spine. "I'm sorry. I didn't mean to… put you off. But no one commands me."

"Tell you what. I'll give you one minute to say whatever it is you need to say, and if I'm not satisfied with it you're going to fry.. What do you think about that?" I hoped my bravado was enough to scare him off. Truth was, I still didn't know how to kill a vampire. But I was the only thing standing between this one and my family, so if it came down to it, I would light his ass up like a Christmas tree. I summoned fire and held it at the ready in the back of my mind.

The vampire didn't flinch, just locked those dark eyes on me while he spoke. "I need your help because I am being hunted. I want no part of what Mallis has planned for your community. And this town is only the beginning. When Mallis brings eternal darkness here, do you think he plans to stop? No, it will spread, engulfing everything in its path. It will be like a plague of locusts, locusts with sharp claws and hungry fangs that will devour everything in their path."

"The Leveling? I know what he has planned for us. It will require big magic. Magic that he doesn't have."

"You are wrong. Why do you think he has not come after you in the past few days?" He looked around and gestured at the ward separating us. "Do you think this would stop him?"

He caught me off guard with that one. I didn't have an answer, but I certainly wasn't about to let him know that. "Yeah. I do."

"False bravado, little witch. But whatever helps you sleep through the night."

Annoyance began to dance around in the back of my mind, and I decided it was time to move this along. "Tick tock *little* vamp," I said. To drive the point home I summoned a flare of magical fire into my hand and held it out in the bloodsucker's direction.

"Fine," he said holding up one hand as if in surrender. "As I said, I'm not here to fight. I couldn't even if I wanted to…Mallis believes he no longer needs you to bring about the Leveling. That is why he has not atacked."

"There haven't been any reports of kidnappings or

disappearances lately. He doesn't have enough witches to power the spell."

"He doesn't need them. He has taken a mate. A witch, and from what I've seen, she is powerful enough on her own."

My stomach churned at his words. Since I don't have balls, I can't really say what it would feel like to be kicked in them, but I think this was probably close. "That's a lie. No witch would betray her kind by doing this."

"Well, one of your type doesn't see that way. I have never met her; only Mallis is allowed to interact with her. Well, he and that Warlock of his. They are always locked away, practicing their magics. From what I have gleaned she is teaching the Warlock and improving his skills in the mystic arts. She is helping him prepare for the Leveling."

I took a slight step forward, not bothering to hide the anger in my eyes. "And how do you know all of this?"

"I was Mallis's...lieutenant at one point. Many years ago, before all of this. He sent for me a few weeks ago, and asked me to resume my position in his new movement."

"So then why are you here? Isn't there supposed to be some type of honor among thieving bloodsuckers?"

He winced visibly at that one, but continued on without missing a beat. "I am not the vampire I once was , said Elion, "the vampire Mallis remembers. When I was a newborn, I was dark and savage. I was a product of my times; easily molded into Mallis's image. But that was long ago, before Mallis left our home for these shores. In the ensuing centuries I have changed. I am not what he remembers, and when I refused to revisit such black memories, he turned on me. Or, more precisely, *she* turned on me, and convinced him I was a threat to his plans."

Something about the way he stood, the way he moved,

made me take a closer look at him. He wasn't standing up completely straight, and though he was visible in pockets of shadow created by my magical flare, I could see that he held one arm across his midsection.

"What's wrong with you?" I was practically right up against the ward and didn't dare cross through it to where he was standing for a closer look.

"After awhile, when Mallis couldn't convince me to join him, and his witch whispered in his ear that I was a threat, he tried to have me taken out. He threw me to his pack of wolves. I had to fight my way clear, and headed to the one place I hoped I could find help: here."

I cocked my head to one side, still eyeing him suspiciously. He responded to my distrust with a nod, then lifted his shirt to reveal long, jagged slashes across his torso. Cuts that were so deep I could see the white flesh beneath the muscle that was torn away. He then turned his back to me, showing deep puncture wounds in a semicircular pattern around his waist and lower back. Wolf bites.

With a wince, he faced me and lowered his top. He started to undo his belt but I stopped him. "No need to show me whatever happened down there. Why aren't you dead?"

"I'm not that easy to kill. But the wounds are very bad; I need to heal. The wolves will be out looking for me once the sun comes up. They know I will have to go to ground somewhere during daylight, I'll be defenseless and weak. That's when they will finish me off."

"So what, they follow you here and take all of us out in the process?"

"You are off-limits to attacks. At least for now," he replied.

"Why? I thought you said Mallis didn't need me anymore."

"I have no idea," said Elion, " but I do know that was an order that was given to the shifters. Perhaps he has back-end plans for you after the Leveling? Who knows. But that is why I came here. The wolves will not try to attack me at night…even wounded, I am still stronger than them. But the daylight is a different matter. No matter where I go, their senses will allow them to track me."

"Why aren't you healing? I thought that was what vampires do."

"I will. In time. But I can't take another mauling from the shifters. Mallis saw what happened to me. He knows I'm not dead."

"Then if he doesn't know where you are now, he will once the shifters track you tomorrow. They will track you right to my doorstep."

"Perhaps. Unless…a witch were to magically cover my trail. Or another type of shifter were to move through the woods in this area, masking my scent with his own very… unique one." He eyed Jhamal once again and received a warning growl in response.

"How are we supposed to trust you? What if I let you onto our property and you decide to go all uber-predator on us and take us all out?"

"I can only give you my word that I have no interest in being that person. As I said, I have changed. Besides, in my current condition I don't think I could survive an attack from your friend there. If it makes you feel better you could simply tether me."

"Tether?"

Now it was the vampire's turn to cock his head in my direction, raising one eyebrow. "You have a lot to learn. And

I will be happy to help you." He could tell I wasn't convinced. "Mallis fears you. I know that much. I can help you to learn about your magic and how to use it against the supernatural creatures that he is calling on, the creatures he is using to lead his charge into the new dark age he longs for. I have lived for over a thousand years, and in that time I have learned a thing or two about magic."

I looked him over again, and he really did look like he was at un-death's door. "How many wolves attacked you?"

"Six," he replied. "They were fast and vicious. Well-trained, they worked as a unit. They were all littermates." He raised his head and sniffed the air. "One has already been here, I see. His scent is all over you."

"What?"

"Whoever you have been with recently is a wolf. And from his scent, I can tell that he is a littermate to the band that serves Mallis now."

Chapter Two

"No. I will not sleep under the same room as...that!" Hope was beside herself, eyes wide and filled with terror at the sight of Elion.

Her reaction was appropriate given the circumstances and everything she had gone through. Honestly, it had been a miracle that my aunts hadn't tried to vaporize Elion on sight when I allowed him through the ward and escorted him to the house.

"Allie, are you mad?" Aunt Vivian had asked, meeting us at the front door. The top deck from which everyone had been watching us had no stair access, so I'd had to march the vampire around the house and to the main entrance.

"He's hurt," I'd said. "And he's not a part of the whole Mallis movement. He says he can help us."

That was when Hope had her freakout moment. "Allie, are you crazy? That thing could be one of the monsters that killed my parents!"

"I assure you I did not," said Elion, calmly taking in the scene he had just created.

Hope marched forward and put a finger in the vampire's face. "Don't you fucking speak to me!"

"Hope, please, let me explain—" I started.

"Nope. Not a chance. I'm outta here." She turned and stormed to the stairs that led to the downstairs guest room that she was using. "I would rather sleep in the park than share a space with...that. I'd have the same chance of making it through the night!"

I followed her, catching up before she reached the stairs. "Hope, listen. You know what we are up against. We were just talking about next steps, right? Well, this just might be part of taking that next step."

"Allie, we were talking about ways to kill that thing and end this nightmare once and for all. And before you can say it, don't tell me 'we weren't trying to figure out how to kill *that* particular monster.' To me, they are all the same."

"Oh yeah? What about Cody? And Jhamal? Do you lump them in with 'all the monsters'?" She swallowed hard and I could see the wheels turning. "Both Cody and Jhamal have risked their lives to save others. Mine included."

"That's different, Allie. They are different, I guess...but you just can't expect me—"

"Hope." I reached out and placed my hand behind her neck, forcing her to meet my eyes. "I made you a promise. I told you I would never let anything happen to you, and I intend to keep that promise. I also said that I wanted you here, where I felt it was safest, and I still mean that. I want you here with my family...the thing that means more to me right now than anything." She smiled and sniffed, rubbing at her eyes. "I know I've said this to you before and maybe you felt like I didn't always live up to it, but you have to trust me. My gut is telling me this is the right thing to do...but I need you onboard and staying under this roof. Okay?"

She hugged me and I could feel her nodding her head. "Fine. But I swear to God, Allie, if I see one fang come my way, it's going to be on!"

I laughed and agreed, but then her countenance turned dark and serious. "What is it?"

"Allie, does he need a coffin to sleep in? Cause that might be pushing it for me."

My face must have registered my confusion. "Honestly, I have no idea. I'm pretty sure that's all just Hollywood nonsense. But why don't we ask?" I hooked my arm through hers and led her back to the main living room.

"Yeah...you can ask. Imma stand over here in the kitchen. Near the garlic."

Aunt Vivian and Aunt Lena were standing together, not taking their eyes off Elion. I could practically hear the hum of magic in the air as they held it at the ready. Jhamal was in human form, standing next to Gar protectively. Both of them looked at me apprehensively.

Taking a deep breath, I did what I do best. I blabbered.

"Okay, let's get it all out. We're witches," I indicated my aunts and myself with a circular sweep of one arm. "Cody and Jhamal are shifters, and Elion is a vampire. By all rights, none of us should be hanging out together. As a matter of fact, we should probably each be working on a way to take out the others. But we aren't. You know why? Because there's another big bad out there that looking to take us *all* out!" I paused, hoping that what I was saying was sinking in. "Mallis is looking to reshape everything that we know, to undo the natural order of life. And we humans are about to slip a couple of rungs down the food chain."

That definitely got everyone's attention. "We need a plan, and I think he" —I pointed at Elion— "might be able to help us with that."

"And if he is tricking us?" said Aunt Lena.

"Then we toss him out into the light of day and fry his ass," said Gar before I could answer.

"Exactly," I replied, smiling at my little brother. I turned my full attention to Elion. "Tonight, you give us a lot of answers as to what is going on with your ex-master, or else in the morning you kiss the sun hello. Got it?"

He didn't answer, but instead focused those dark eyes on me.

"I'm going to need you to acknowledge that in the affirmative," I said, undaunted by the intensity of his glare.

"I understand," he said, "and I agree to your terms. I will help you, if you will help me."

"You mentioned something about tethering you," I said. "What is that?"

"Allie, no…" said Aunt Lena.

"Why? What is it?" I asked.

"It's simple," said Elion. "You bind me to a spell of your choosing, one that will most likely result in my destruction, and tether the spell to your life-force. That way, the spell becomes a failsafe. If I attack you, the spell still…detonates It also assures that I do no harm to any of your family or friends, as you can remotely trigger the spell at will."

"Allie, don't even think about it," repeated Aunt Lena. "Those spells are far more dangerous than they appear. Dangerous for the witch that casts them."

I thought about what she was saying. "But it also ensures he can't hurt any of you, right?"

"Yes, but there is a reason why this is called 'tethering,'" said Aunt Vivian. "This is a death spell. In order for it to work post-mortem, you have to link your life-force to this creature. It is a form of black magic that can tarnish a witch forever."

"Well," said Elion, "it is more gray than black."

My aunt gave him a look that would have dropped a charging rhino in its tracks.

"But I have given you my word that I will harm no one under this roof," said Elion. "If you prefer to leave our arrangement at the gentleman's handshake level, you have nothing to worry about."

Something about the way he said "under this roof" bothered me. I wasn't sure why, but it made me think of the old cautionary tale of the spider inviting the spy into its web.

I took out my phone and fired off a quick text to Cody. If a vampire was sleeping under my roof, I'd feel a lot more comfortable having a werewolf here as well. Hopefully a wolf and a totem shifter would provide as much a deterrent as a tethering spell.

"There's one thing we haven't addressed," said Aunt Vivian.

"What's that?" I said.

"He's hurt. Badly. I can feel it when I get close to him."

Elion cocked his head to one side and regarded my aunt with a cool detachment.

"I have already given you my word," he said.

"What are we talking about here?" I asked.

"She is concerned that need to heal," Elion said, "and the quickest way for a vampire to heal is an infusion of new blood."

All heads turned towards the vampire at that statement, and then swiveled back to me.

"Ah, hell no," said Hope, holding one hand protectively against her throat and backing away from the group. "Allie, for a family of witches, why do y'all not have any crosses in this place!" She was looking frantically around at all the knick-knacks that decorated the mantle and end tables in the room.

"Oh, that wouldn't work anyway," said Elion. "That's an old wives' tale made up by desperate old women to make them feel safer in God's hands while their husbands were away."

The matter-of-fact way in which he made the statement caused me to focus my attention on him. "Alright then. Other than magic, what *will* kill a vampire? I mean, if you want us to trust you, show us your underbelly."

He regarded for the slightest of moments. I could practically hear him deliberating how to answer the question.

"Well, sunlight will do the trick for almost all of us. I say 'almost' because there are some of us that are so old that rumor has it they are now immune. Beheading can also work, though I will warn you that we are very fast and capable of dodging most blows. Bleeding us out and then entombing us in solid earth with no way of escaping can do the trick. Though, that takes a very long time, because even without blood in our systems, a part of us can still be alive, even after decades. But again, a word of caution: if that emaciated corpse does rise, it will forever be a different kind of vampire, a rabid beast with hungers that you cannot begin to imagine. Severe wounds…like the ones I possess… can weaken us to the point that we are susceptible to death from brute force. In my weakened state I would not survive another encounter with those werewolves. Or a…lion," he glanced at Jhamal. "May I ask…what are you?"

"You may not," said Gar moving to stand between his boyfriend and those piercing black eyes.

Elion arched a single eyebrow and nodded. "I see. Other than that, magic is our greatest enemy. Witches have the power to un-make us."

My ears pricked up at this. "How? What do you mean 'un-make' you?"

"I don't know *how* they do it, if that's what you're asking. It's very old magic. Personally, I have only seen it done once before, and to be honest, I have no desire to ever see something like that again."

"What about a stake to the heart?" asked Hope, calling from the comfort of the kitchen.

"That would probably only piss us off. I myself have never been staked, but I can only imagine it would do little to truly harm me. My heart doesn't beat, after all, so there is very little that will damage it further."

"So...if your heart doesn't beat, what do you need to drink blood for? How does it circulate?" I asked.

"Blood acts as an internal lubricant, for lack of a better phrase," Elion replied. "Our hearts do not beat, but the blood is still always being absorbed into the tissues and muscles of our bodies. Without it, we will eventually cease to move, becoming living statues. Although, that takes centuries to happen."

"You mean that one day, if you don't get enough to drink, you just...rust solid?" asked Hope.

"It would have to be a conscious decision," he said. "We have the ability to subsist on as little as a few drops of blood per week. Unless we are injured, that is. So in order to become locked into our own bodies, we must make the decision to stop drinking blood completely."

"Have you ever seen this?" said Aunt Vivian.

"Yes. In the old country I heard tales of vampires so old they grew tired of living. So they stopped drinking and became living fossils. I have only seen one such creature, but yes, it can happen."

My aunt didn't say anything else but I could see her

brow furrow as her gaze lost its focus, the way it does when it was family game night and we were playing an especially competitive game of gin. I gave her a questioning look but she just waved me off and moved to stand next to Aunt Lena.

"So back to our original question," said Hope. "How are you going to heal without blood?"

"Time," replied Elion. "I just need uninterrupted time where I don't have to stress myself. I will heal on my own, but that can't happen if I am running for my life or fighting off shifters."

"Why don't you just drink the blood of the shifters that are attacking you?" asked Gar.

"Shifter blood is not the same as human blood. We were once human, so that blood is what drives us. Shifters are more animal than you might think; their blood is of little use to us. It can be done, but it's like trying to force an unleaded vehicle to run on leaded fuel."

"What is leaded fuel?" asked Gar.

"Not the time or the place," I replied to him. I turned to face Elion. "So you want to lay low here, shielded by our magic until you're back to full strength? And then…?"

"And then I will help you defeat Mallis. I don't want to see his plans come to fruition anymore than you do."

"And why is that?" asked Aunt Lena. "Surely an eternal night would appeal to all vampires."

"No. Rest assured, not all of us would like that."

Something told me he wanted to say more but didn't bother to elaborate.

"Even if we bought that story, I don't think you'll be that much of a help to us," I said. "We seem to be doing just fine on our own."

I could tell immediately that he knew I was lying, but I kept my chin held high in defiance.

"Perhaps," he said. "But you have no idea what you are up against. He has new allies."

"So you said," I responded. "A new witch in his circle. Well, I'm not afraid of a witch." This was nothing but the truth, and I hoped he could tell.

"It is not the witch I speak of," he said, his black eyes boring into me. "He has a new shifter at his disposal. A hellhound."

Just then, the door opened and Cody walked in. Immediately he stiffened at the sight of Elion. His eyes began to glow yellow as his started to shift into his hybrid wolf form.

"Someone mind telling me what the hell a vampire is doing in this house?" he said, his voice guttural and low.

Chapter Three

"Allie, what the hell?!" I could feel the anger rolling off of him.

He stepped forward, body tense, fists clenched. I met him before he could get too far into the room quickly, placing one hand on his chest.

"Easy Cody," I said. "Let's take it down a notch...er...a shift."

He growled low and mumbled something I didn't catch, but at least he shifted back to full human form, although I did notice that he kept his claws.

His eyes narrowed as they lit on Elion. "Okay. So anyone care to let me know what's going on?"

Surprisingly it only took a matter of minutes to give him the gist of what was happening. Not surprisingly, he didn't trust Elion's story in the least.

"So everything goes quiet for over a week now. No sign of Mallis or his wolves. But now, with the eclipse less than a week away, you just happen to show up needing 'help' and asking for asylum. Yeah, right."

"I've told your friends everything…" began Elion.

"Yeah, right. Sure you have," said Cody.

"Cody, stop," I implored. "The fact is, he's hurt. No faking that. I felt his pain with my magic. He's offering us his aid. And he's bringing us information that we need."

"Allie," Cody said, wheeling to face me, "ever hear of the Trojan horse before?"

I had nothing to say, but Gar apparently did. "He's got a point, Allie. You sent me and our aunts away from here because you were afraid of what could happen to us at the hands of Mallis and his army. Yet, now you're ready to invite one in to our midst? And not just any one of them; one of his *generals*, from the sound of it."

Elion cut a glance in Gar's direction and I again noticed how Jhamal moved protectively closer to him. "I will leave. I can see what my presence here has wrought." He moved to head towards the door but I stopped him.

"No. If the things you are saying are true, then we will need all the help we can get. I'm listening to my gut here, and guys, I have to tell you, I'm not getting any warning signs off him at all." I turned to face my family and friends, imploring them to think things through. "And honestly, if he's feeling better in a couple of days and starts to give off creepster vibes, then…"

"Then what?" Gar asked.

"Then I'll feed him to the wolves my damn self," I finished.

"Wait…you're going to make Cody eat him?" Gar exclaimed.

"What? No, Gar…I was just using that as an example. He knows what I mean." I gave Elion my most sinister look, and in return, the bastard just smiled at me.

"Something is burning," he said.

"What…?" I looked around for a moment before it hit me. Shit! I ran into the kitchen and flung open the oven door. Fanning at the smoke that greeted me, I grabbed a kitchen mat and reached into the oven to retrieve my collapsed, smoldering, black soufflés.

Awesomesauce. And speaking of, the orange sauce was stuck to the bottom of the pan. There was no saving it so I lifted it off the burner and placed it in the sink. Both the ramekins and the saucepan would have to be thrown out, and for some reason that pissed me off even more than having that bloodsucking ghoul standing in our home.

I stalked out of the kitchen, right up to Elion.

"Okay here's the deal. You can stay, but under these conditions: tell us everything you know about Mallis and your relationship with him, past and present. Give us everything on the witch he has as his new love interest and how the Warlock fits into all of this. If you know anything about the Leveling and how to stop it, I want that as well. Lastly, I need to know all the ways possible to kill Mallis."

Elion looked at me and blinked, but then slowly nodded his head.

"Also, you'll stay under lock and key—mystically speaking of course—while you're here. You don't step foot outside of the room we place you in unless you want to fry, got it?" Again, he nodded. "And no biting any of my friends. No matter how hungry you get."

"I'm standing guard outside his room," Cody said. He whirled to face me before I could complain. "No questioning that, Allie. You have your conditions, and I have mine."

"I'm standing watch, too," said Jhamal looking over at Cody. "If he blinks wrong, we split him in two."

An uncomfortable silence was broken by Aunt Vivian

when she cleared her throat. "Now that we have all of that settled, tell us more about this hellhound that Mallis has."

All eyes were on Elion as he turned to address my aunt. "There isn't much I can tell you. I have never seen one prior to this; in truth, I didn't believe they existed. But he has one now."

"Wait—is that what attacked you?" Gar asked.

"No. Mallis is still learning to control the hound. I was attacked by werewolves."

"So what exactly is a hellhound?" asked Hope, easing her way closer to the group.

"It's a shifter that was born in another realm. A dimension of demons rather than humans. In that realm there are beings that are capable of taking on nightmarish forms. This particular shifter can transform into a dog that is far larger than a werewolf. While it retains the same physical characteristics of a dog, as the name suggests, its body is covered in the fires of hell...or so we were led to believe. Red flames that burn cold give the beast its name."

"Cold fire? How does that work?" asked Gar.

Elion shook his head. "I don't know that, but I do know that the flames, though cold, can still burn through most substances in this realm. I saw that creature melt a human being down to a pile of slag in a matter of seconds."

The room went quiet and all I could think was, *Great, one more monster to kill.* I needed to break the silence. "Where did he find it?"

"His witch has been experimenting with opening dimensional portals and was able to coax it over to our side," Elion said. "It's part of their preparation for the Leveling."

This caught everyone's attention.

"What part does this play?" said Aunt Lena.

"Surely you didn't think that simply bringing about eternal darkness was Mallis' final play, did you?" said Elion.

"Yes," I said, "because that would allow him to move freely in our town without the fear of becoming a living roman candle. You mean there is more?"

"Freedom of movement and the ability to feed at will are part of it. But what he truly wants is power…power over other supernaturals. The kind of control he seeks is not easily obtained. He does not want to simply become the defect leader of supernaturals; he wants them bent to his will completely. And once that happens, he will spread his war from your town to the entire world."

"That's crazy," I said. "He wants dominion over a world that is run by non-human creatures?"

"Exactly," said Elion. "He wants things returned to the old ways. The order of things prior to the rise of man and the beginnings of documented history. In those days, the Earth was part of the Fae Lands. There was no light…only eternal darkness. Vampires ruled every living creature and had complete domination of the planet. Other species existed to be slaves, soldiers, food…or some combination of the three."

"This is madness," said Aunt Lena. "I have never heard of such a time."

"Of course you haven't. It predates humans."

"If that's true, then what happened?" asked Hope.

"There was a mystical Big Bang, if you will. And from that bang came mankind. And from mankind appeared the first witches. They were capable of doing something that the vampires could not."

"Magic," whispered Aunt Vivian.

Elion nodded. "That is correct. The first witches took it upon themselves to route the darkness—to make this plane safe for humans. And because there were not ,many practitioners of magic at the time, they had the vast magical reserves of an entire planet to tap into, and that allowed them to perform great feats that have dwarfed any that have come after them."

"Wait," said Aunt Vivian. "I'm pretty up-to-date on my lore, and I have never heard it said that witches share a single source of magic, that the more witches there are, the less magic there is to go around."

"Why do you think that true witches are born?" said Elion. "There are many humans running around practicing the craft, and attempting to cast spells, but for the majority it's all smoke and mirrors. Not the real thing. Not like the magic that is available to families that are born into it; families such as this one."

"If that's true," said Aunt Lena, "then do you expect us to believe that one day magic will simply disappear; that it will be used up?"

"Yes. One day, your kind will have tapped the last reserves of a dwindling pool. And when that day comes, hell will follow behind it." My aunts stared at the floor in silence, too shocked to speak. "Of course, who knows when that day will be? It might be tomorrow, it might be next week, or it might be a thousand years from now. But it will come eventually. Unfortunately, Mallis is not a patient vampire. He does not want to wait for the natural order to play out; he wants to leapfrog ahead and make that day happen now."

And there it was. The endgame.

"So Mallis wants to not only take out the sun, but remove magic from this world as well?" I said. "And no more magic means no more witches."

"And when that happens, he has no more enemies. He will truly be at the top of the food chain," said Aunt Vivian.

"I still say it's not possible," began Aunt Lena, "the amount of magic it would take…"

"Is something that he is accounting for," said Elion. "That is why his witch has been experimenting with opening portals to the darker realms. She wants to tap into the black power that fuels that realm; combine it with what she can draw on here. Between the two realms, a single witch could obtain enough power to create the Leveling." He paused, seeming to hold his breath slightly.

"What is it?" I asked, catching his reluctance.

"If she taps into the dark magic of that realm, it will leave a marker. Footprints, if you will…"

"Footprints that will lead back to this world," I finished.

He nodded. "And if there is one thing that denizens of dark dimensions love, it's finding new dimensions to spread to."

"Well surely Mallis has thought of that," said Cody. "I mean, that seems obvious to me. If he has everything planned out to this degree, then I'm betting he wants this crossover to happen as well."

"Makes sense," said Gar. "Maybe he plans on sharing this world."

Elion looked at my brother and recognition seemed to spread over his features. "Yes, of course. The Leveling will break many of the natural laws of nature. It will allow supernaturals that are banished from this plane to return. But if he tears open a portal to an entirely new demon dimension—and that's what we are talking about—then it introduces a whole new class of supernaturals for him to subjugate. Creatures like that hellhound."

We were all silent as the vampire's words sunk in. The

scope of what he was saying boggled my mind. Even my aunts weren't speaking.

"Maybe you're right," said Hope, looking at my aunts, "maybe it can't be done. I mean, I can barely wrap my head around the idea of this being real. Maybe it's not even possible."

"Oh, I assure you it's possible," said Elion. "When Mallis learned that the Forbidding was erected, he began to research what it would take to bring about the Leveling."

"The Forbidding," I said, snapping to attention. "What does that have to do with this?"

"Two sides of the same magic," he replied. "When Mallis realized that there was a witch out there powerful enough to erect the Forbidding, then he knew that somewhere there had to be one that could do the opposite… bring the world back to the time when shadows, and the things that crept within them, ruled."

"Are there any vampires left that remember that time?" asked Aunt Vivian.

Elion shook his head. "If there are, they have long ago stopped moving and turned to stone."

"Okay," I said. "All of this doesn't change anything. We will take your words under advisement, but you still sleep guarded and warded."

Elion nodded his understanding.

"I'll show you to a space in the basement. Technically, it's a storage room but there are no windows for you to worry about come sun-up. I'll get you a cot and blanket…if you get cold, that is."

"Thank you," he said. I was surprised by how sincere he sounded. "One last thing before I retire, however."

"Look buddy, you're in no place to make any requests," said Cody.

Elion looked at him, his black eyes narrowing. "Not a request, a warning. You may want to keep your boyfriend out of this fight." He looked from me to Cody, ignoring the rest of the room.

"What? You're crazy if you think I'm sitting this out," replied Cody.

"Yeah, that's not happening," I said. "What makes you think that's even an option?"

Elion seemed genuinely confused by my answer. "Because he's one of them."

"One of who? A werewolf? We know that..." Gar said.

"No, not just a werewolf. He's a member of the pack of wolves that attacked me, the ones that are loyal to Mallis."

"What are you talking about?" I said, feeling a cold sweat run down my spine.

"He is a littermate of the wolves that attacked me. They were all siblings, and this one"—he pointed at Cody—"is one of them. They all have the same smell...and it is coming off of him as well. If there is one thing I know about werewolves, their bond is stronger than...magic," he said glancing my way. "And eventually, they always turn on anyone that is not their blood."

Chapter Four

Needless to say, I didn't sleep well that night.

I tossed and turned, lying awake and staring at the ceiling fan as it whirred along in my room. I could hear footsteps throughout the night padding to the kitchen, the slight *whoosh* and *pop* as the refrigerator door was opened and closed, dishes being taken out of the cabinets, and water running.

Apparently, no one was quite ready to fall into a deep slumber with a vampire in the house. Even though my aunts and I assured everyone that the wards were impregnable by Elion, I could tell my friends were still uncomfortable.

True to their word, Cody and Jhamal took up positions on the floor just outside of the storage room where Elion resided. Cody had put on a big pot of coffee, and the two of them were stubbornly downing cup after cup and chatting quietly to one another. Even though I wanted to tell them they were being ridiculous, I was secretly a little relieved they were there. Magic or no, I had no idea what a vampire was capable of, and didn't want to find out the hard way in the middle of the night.

The house was silent when I got out of bed, just before dawn. It was my turn to make my way to the kitchen and brew a strong pot of coffee. The steaming cup felt good in my hands as I headed out onto the deck to enjoy the sunrise. I wasn't too surprised to find Aunt Lena sitting on the sofa, a bright teal throw wrapped around her slender frame.

"No tea?" I asked. It was strange seeing her without her special brew of herbs steeping away in a porcelain mug.

"No, not today. I haven't slept and I don't need anything with even a hint of caffeine in it."

"I don't think anyone slept last night."

"Can you blame them?" She turned to face me as I sat down beside her.

"Do you think I've made a mistake, Aunt Lena?"

She sighed, pursing her lips together tightly before speaking. "Allie. I can't tell you that. With what we are up against, I agree that we need all the help we can get. Would I, in my day, have offered asylum to a vampire? Never. But these are different times. And you're a different kind of witch."

Her words were meant to calm me, but they didn't work. I sipped from the mug, enjoying the feel of the hot liquid making its way through my body, warming me and providing just the right amount of energy to start to feel like myself.

"I know it sounds weird, but I just *feel* the this is the right thing to do," I said.

"And that's enough for your aunt and I. Witches must always their instincts."

"But something about this still bothers you, right?"

She sighed and smiled at me. "It isn't the vampire locked in the basement that makes me nervous, although your aunt might argue that point; rather, it's everything he told us."

I crossed my legs and sat facing her, leaning in with my cup between us. "Do you believe everything he said?"

She nodded slowly. "I do, Allie. And that terrifies me. What he is saying rewrites the history books on witches and magic. Quite frankly, the fact that a vampire knows more about our history than we do scares me. What else is going on of which we are blissfully unaware?"

I knew what she meant, and yet I wasn't sure how to comfort her.

"There's something else, Allie," she continued. "This witch that he speaks of— Mallis's new lover—who is she and where did she come from? If she is as powerful as Elion claims, then how did she make her way into town without us knowing about her? Magical markers that bright aren't easy to shield."

"Maybe it's someone that was already here?"

Aunt Lena shook her head. "Not possible. We would know if there was another witch like that in town. No, something is just not right about this."

"You sound like Gar. Do you think Elion is lying to us?"

She thought about this for a moment before answering. "No. I am sure he is telling us everything that he knows about the situation. I just think there are other aspects that have been kept from him."

We sat there in silence as I sipped my coffee. Finally, I looked at her and said, "You realize that in order for us to have a chance at winning this, we need help, right?"

She sighed and smiled. "Yes. But keep both eyes open around that vampire, Allie."

"I'm not talking about the vampire, Aunt Lena."

She frowned and couldn't hold my gaze. "Allie, I don't know about trying that…even your Aunt Vivian thinks it's a bad idea."

"Aunt Lena, please," I implored. "Even with Kendra and the rest of the shifters in town, we can't stand up to an army of supernaturals and an entire pack of werewolves. We need more shifters to stand with us."

"And you think Totem Shifters are the answer?"

"You saw the way Elion kept looking at Jhamal. He wasn't sure what he was. And he said that in his weakened state Jhamal would have no trouble finishing him off. I think he feared not knowing what Jhamal was…well, at least as much as he could fear anything, I guess. So it's the only option we have."

"Allie, we don't even know how Jhamal was created."

"His aunt said that he was given a totem, his necklace, and that was what allowed him to reach the creature that lived within him…his true self. His abilities are based in magic."

"So you want to reverse engineer that magic and create more like him?"

"It's worth a try. Without more supernaturals, we can't win. And if we lose…"

"Yes. I know what that means."

"Then help me. Between the three of us, we should be able to figure out the magic that unlocked totem shifting and recreate it. I'm a Reliquary! I have all of this power inside of me that you said I could tap into to create wonders. What good is having the power if I don't use it for something that can save the world? My mother used her power to lock evil away from the world of man, saving countless lives. Maybe I inherited her powers so that I can do the same thing for my generation? Maybe I'm meant to make a grand gesture that not only saves mankind but helps people in the process? Jhamal told me how much pain he was in before he could reach his totem—before he could make himself whole. How many more people are out there like him? Just waiting for someone to make them whole."

I stopped, swallowing hard. Aunt Lena reached over and took my hand in hers.

"You're a good person, Allie. Don't ever forget that. Your aunt and I will do what we can to help you. But like you said, you're the Reliquary. We don't have the power to make such things a reality." She reached up and cupped my chin in her hand and turned me to face her. "I'm proud of you. We are going to get through this, and you want to know how I know that?"

"Magic?"

She laughed, her eyes lighting up with joy. "No, child. Because someone like you is meant to do great things. Not die at the hand of some crazed vampire and his haggard witch of a lover."

And just like that, everything felt right in the world again. I set my coffee down and rested my head on her shoulder.

"I'm afraid, Aunt Lena."

"That's a good thing. It means you feel the weight of just how serious this is. It means you realize just what all you stand to lose in this fight. Use that fear to help make you stronger. Something tells me you're going to have to make some hard decisions in the next couple of days, but I know you'll do the right thing."

I looked up at her, intending to respond. But then,

before I could get anything out, I felt the deck begin to sway beneath me. The sky tilted towards the ground and I felt the sudden urge to vomit. Then, everything went black, and I started to fall.

Chapter Five

I felt myself falling deeper than the deck should have allowed. My aunt was screaming into the darkness and calling out my name. No matter how badly I wanted to reach up to her, I couldn't. My body was frozen...and yet falling at the same time. The blackness around me was suffocating; my own screams were sucked away by the vacuum that I was suddenly trapped within.

Cody's voice broke through the pitch and reached my ears.

"Allie! Allie! What's wrong with her?" he was screaming.

"I don't know," said Aunt Lena. "She just got this weird look on her face and then went out. Someone get a pillow to put under her head!"

Her voice was starting to sound farther away, like it was coming from the end of a tunnel that was getting longer. The darkness was pressing in around me, making it more and more difficult to breathe, and my inner self was the verge of a full-blown panic attack.

What the hell was happening to me? I still felt like I was

falling, deeper and deeper into quick sand. But according to what I was hearing, my body was probably lying on the deck. I've fainted before, from physical exertion in gym class during the heat of summer. But this was totally different. So…how was this happening?

Magic. That was what I needed. To grab onto my magic and get myself out of here. I focused, making myself slow my breathing as I reached for the mystic fire that simmered within me. I would stoke it, call it forth…use it to blast my way out of…wherever I was. I would…do nothing. There was nothing there…no magic spark of any kind.

Okay, maybe panicking wasn't such a bad idea.

I could hear my breathing suddenly became slow and more forceful, rattling the space around me. At least I assumed it was my breathing…but my physical body was not here. Which meant I *wouldn't* be able to hear my breath. *So if I'm not the one breathing like that, then who—or what—is?*

Weightless and in complete darkness, orientation meant nothing to me. Was I face-up, down, sideways? I had no way of knowing and therefore no way of knowing where the sound was coming from. I listened closer: it was a huff with sharp exhalations, followed by a low growl. Now, *that* was a sound I was familiar with. Werewolf.

Suddenly, the wolf was beside me, below me, in front of me…it was everywhere at once. Somehow, without making a sound, it padded up to me until it was inches from my face. Vertigo had me spinning almost uncontrollably, but no matter what direction I ended up in, there it was: fangs and yellow eyes to my face.

It opened its mouth and I was sure it was about to bite me, but instead, it spoke.

"Allie," it growled, "it's so nice to meet you in person."

The fear I felt before skyrocketed to heights I had never

dreamt of. Since when the hell do these things speak while in *animal form?*

"Oh we've always been able to speak," said the wolf, noting my surprise, "it's just that for the most part we choose not to. Oh, and in case you're wondering about the fact that I just read your mind…yeah, we hang out in here a lot, when possible."

Where's here? I thought.

"The space between. The fold between worlds. The no-dawn. Or you may know it simply as The Grey. I probably shouldn't be telling you all of this, but you'll be dead in a matter of minutes so it really doesn't matter."

I felt/saw/heard the wolf move even closer to me. Again, it opened its jaws, snaking a long red tongue out to lick delicately at my face. Jesus, I could *feel* the sandpapery bit of flesh on me! It was not smooth like a normal canine; more feline-esque if anything.

"This place is foreign to you," continued the wolf. "Your magic has abandoned you. No friends coming to your rescue this time. Just you and me— finally."

Fuck you, monster! You don't know me. If you're going to kill me please just shut up and get it over with!

A dry chuckle filled the space around my ears. "Such an eager little witch. And you're wrong; I do know you. I know you oh so well…I wouldn't be here if it weren't for you."

And just like that, I knew. Just as the creature opened his mouth, showing fangs that I knew could sever my neck in a single bite, I knew.

I knew who the thing was, and the shock of that knowledge catapulted me into action.

No way was I dying at the hands—er jaws—of any supernatural. I had made a promise to people that I loved, and I was damned sure going to keep it. Summoning all of the inner reserves I had, I screamed and lashed out at the werewolf with all the strength I had. Although I couldn't feel my arms or legs, I willed them to strike, propelling the beast away from me. Somehow, that primal urge to survive struck a mystical nerve inside me and my magic flared to life.

Blue light and familiar heat flashed all around me. I gathered it and channeled it outward at the wolf, his howl matching my screams. I struck with everything inside me, commanding my magic to suffocate the darkness.

And just like that, I opened my eyes to find myself staring up at the ceiling in my aunts' living room.

"What happened?" I asked, sitting up a little too fast. The room began to spin around me and for one panicked moment I thought I was falling back into the darkness.

"It's okay, Allie," said Aunt Vivian taking me by the hand. "You're back and everything is fine now."

Looking around, it took me a moment to recognize the room I was in. The coffee table and end tables were upturned, the area rug was singed and smoking, and nearly all of the little knick-knacks on the now smashed display shelves were in ruins.

"What...oh my God, what happened?"

"You did," said Gar. That was when I noticed that he, Hope, and Jhamal were standing far away from me. The look in Hope's eyes scared me as much as the place I had just been lost in.

"I did this?" I put one hand on my head, trying to steady my reeling senses.

"Just relax," said Aunt Vivian, trying to gently press me back into a reclined position. "Your aunt and I felt the swell of magic inside you before the release. We were able to get a shield up around everyone. No one was hurt."

Yeah, at least not physically. I couldn't bring myself to look at Hope again. My aunt's hand felt warm in mine as I gave her a slight squeeze. Thankfully, they had been here when this happened.

"How did I get in here?" I asked. "The last thing I remember was being outside on the deck with Aunt Lena."

"She called for help when you collapsed, dear. Cody was kind enough to carry you inside and place you on the couch."

Cody!

Against my aunts' wishes I sat up, looking around for my boyfriend. At the same instant, he walked into the room with a cold compress and rushed to my side when he saw I was awake.

"I asked him to get a cold cloth for your head after you came out of…whatever was happening to you," said Aunt Vivian. "Allie, what happened?"

"I…I'm not sure," I said, staring at Cody. "But wherever I just got sucked into, you were there. Or rather, your wolf was there."

"What do you mean?" he responded. "I haven't left the house, Allie."

"I know. Like I said, it wasn't you the *man*, but it was definitely you the *wolf*. I have no idea how that would be possible."

Aunt Lena sat down next to me on the couch. "Allie, where were you? What do you remember?"

"I remember everything, Aunt Lena. We were on the deck talking, and suddenly, out of nowhere, it felt like I was passing out. Only without the losing-consciousness part. Everything went dark and I was falling, only I didn't feel myself hitting the deck. I just kept falling, through everything, and into this pitch black nothingness that seemed like it wanted to swallow me whole. At first I could hear you calling to me, and then...I heard other voices as well. They sounded so far away, and I couldn't answer back. I just kept falling. I even heard you, Cody..."

"Lena," said Aunt Vivian, "did you notice anything strange when it happened?"

"No," replied my aunt. "Like she said, one minute we were talking, and the next she was out cold. I did feel a slight...shiver almost, pass through her body, but it was so brief that I didn't think anything of it. I certainly didn't feel any type of malevolent magics at work around her."

"You said my wolf was there," said Cody. "Like you were dreaming, or do you mean...literally?"

"It wasn't a dream. The fear I felt was way too real. I was falling, and I couldn't make heads or tails of which way was what. Everything seemed to meld together. I even tried using my magic, but there was nothing there; nothing worked. But then I heard breathing coming at me from all sides. Then a growl, that unmistakable growl of a shifter. It was close, until all at once it appeared in front of me: a werewolf. It spoke to me—"

"I'm sorry, it spoke?" said Aunt Vivian. "Are you certain?"

"As certain as I can be about anything that just happened. But I wasn't imagining it, that I know. It said it knew me and everyone else up here. It told me it was there to kill me, and that this time there would be no friends to save me. I believed it...it meant to end my life. And its voice, its eyes..." I shivered at the memory and gripped my aunt's hand tighter, "it was you, Cody...and that final realization, just as you were about to bite me, filled me with so much fear that I lashed out with everything I had. Next thing I knew, I was here."

"Could she have been astral projecting?" asked Aunt Lena.

"Possibly," said Aunt Vivian. "Her description is what one would expect from an unprepared witch on her first venture into the astral plane. But...why would she have encountered anything there that meant her harm? The astral plane is a place of spiritual awakening."

My eyes widened as I remembered something else. "The Grey! Cody...er...the wolf, told me the place we were in was called The Grey. He said it didn't matter if I knew or not because I would be dead soon."

"The Grey?" said Gar. "Do you know what that means?" I could only shake my head.

"The Grey is the space that resides between this world and that of the supernaturals." We all turned at the sound of Elion's voice to see him standing in the doorway that led from the main level to the basement. "It's a no man's land. A place where spirits walk."

"How are you up and about in the daylight?" said Aunt Lena.

"More importantly, how did you get out of that warded room?" added Cody angrily.

"I am perfectly capable of moving about during daytime as long as I am not in direct sunlight," he said, glancing around him. Where he stood, no light from the windows reached and I noticed that he was careful to make no movements to indicate that he might try to step into the main area of the house. "As for the wards, I felt them dissipate moments ago. All of them." His voice was pointed and directed at me.

"Right," said Aunt Vivian. "They must have been taken out when Allie came to. Lena, I'll go restore the ones around the property line. You watch him." With that, she left the room and headed up the stairs towards the large study that they used as a home office-cum-sanctum.

"I'll go with you," said Hope, hurrying after her. She clearly would have preferred to be anywhere than in the same room as Elion.

"Elion, do you know what just happened to Allie?" said Aunt Lena.

The vampire nodded before speaking. "I know where she was, but how it happened, I can only guess. Your aunt was partially correct, what happened to you was akin to astral projection. Your spiritual self left your physical body and traveled to The Grey. In there, your astral form was as vulnerable to attack as your physical body is here."

"You mean, if I had died there..." I began.

"Yes. You would have also died here. That's why your boyfriend's wolf attacked you there. You are inexperienced in the ways of astral projection, making you far easier to eliminate there in The Grey than in this world."

"But I don't have a clue how to astral project," I said. "And if I did, trust me, I would not have gone to that place."

"That's the interesting part," said Elion. "That was a very specific destination, one that I have never heard of a mortal visiting before. If you don't know how to free your astral self, then that can only mean one thing."

My arched eyebrows in his direction told to continue, but Aunt Lena spoke up before he could.

"You didn't leave your body of your own free will," she said. "You were pulled out of yourself and taken to that realm. Someone hijacked you."

"That takes considerable power," said Aunt Vivian from the stairs. She was making her way back down and stoped at the bottom landing with Hope. "To completely wrench someone free of their physical self and hurl them into another dimension without their consent…I've never seen magic like that before."

"It is certainly beyond anything we are capable of," said Aunt Lena.

"It is blood magic," said Elion. "In my younger days as a fledgling vampire, I heard stories of such power. To cast someone's soul out of their body like that requires power and blood."

"What do you mean, 'blood'?" I asked.

"I mean, someone is working some big-time magic over Allie, and they are using her own blood to do it. That's the only way something like that could have happened."

I placed a hand on my throat, feeling for the tiny bite marks that were a parting gift from Mallis. "He, Mallis, bit me…bled me almost completely out. What if her saved some of my blood? Saved it for that witch he is with now?"

Elion nodded slowly. "Yes, that could do it. Maybe."

"Maybe? You just said what happened to me was powered by my blood…what maybe is there to that?"

"Again, I am not schooled in the ways of your magic. I only know what I have heard. Witches are a natural enemy of vampires, so we make it a point to know as much about them as possible. What I am telling you are things that were told to me generations ago."

"And what about me being there?" said Cody. "How was that possible?"

"Now, that I can't help you with," said Elion. "I have never been in The Grey myself, so I don't know what resides there."

"So what now?" I asked, not directed at any one person in particular.

"It's obvious," said Cody. "If Mallis and his witch

concocted this plan, then they are stepping it up to take you out of the picture. Maybe that's why they've been so quiet lately…they were putting everything they had into this one play."

"Perhaps," said Aunt Vivian. "But it seems too…anticlimactic for them. Also, if that were the case, why not attack Allie when she was alone? My bet is they did this to see what would happen, see what your vulnerabilities are."

"If that is true, then you need to strike back quicker than you had planned," said Elion.

"Why's that?" I asked.

"Because there are a host of other, more horrible spells that can be worked with blood magic. And if they have your blood, they will definitely lash out at you with it again."

Fuck. That's just great.

"Well, in that case, I don't have any more time to waste. We need help." I looked at my aunts with determined eyes. "Time to whip us up a new batch of Totem Shifters."

Chapter Six

Thank God Gar was around.

I liked to think that I knew my way around a computer but I was all thumbs when it came to posting what I was looking for across social media.

"Trust me," he had said, "it's not called the Front Page of the Internet for nothing. I'll start a thread, and I guarantee you'll find what you're looking for."

And he was right. I got everything I was looking for and then some. The next six hours were spent sorting through a lot of disturbing replies to the topic "Are You Otherkin?" to find the ones that I felt were worth digging into. Many of the replies recounted moments that these Otherkin had been attacked by "regular" people—apparently in some circles, being Otherkin was a social trigger. I was happy that Gar had thought to create a "throwaway" account for a one-time-use. I just didn't get all the hate. Why couldn't people just stay in their lane and mind their business?

But they were there. So many people identified as Otherkin, normal human beings who self identified as non-human. They believed themselves to be partially or totally an animal or some other mythological beast trapped in a human body. They lived on the fringes of society and were often ridiculed and attacked for believing they were different. My heart broke as I read account after account of people being ridiculed and ostracized because they felt different from mainstream society. They were young, old, black, white, straight, gay and bisexual; it didn't matter to the internet bullies who seemed to live to heckle them. The more I read, the more my heart broke for these people.

By looking at their profiles, I learned that there were a surprising number of Otherkin within a few hours' drive of Trinity Cove, and even more that were within a quick flight or train ride. I returned messages to the ones who I thought fit what I was looking for, and was happy to learn that many of them knew of Trinity Cove. Apparently, word had spread about my small town outside of a Queen City in North Carolina. A town where you could not only be yourself, but maybe, just maybe, you could become something more.

"How does everyone know about us?" I asked Gar.

"Word spreads quickly in certain channels on the internet," he replied. "Witches are talking, as well as some supernaturals. Word also spread from a lot of the humans that are packing up and leaving this town as quickly as they can."

Of course that made sense. If I had to hightail it out of Dodge because there was a chance I might be eaten, then I sure as hell would also be warning anyone that might listen about moving here.

But that didn't seem to deter the Otherkin when I told them I wanted to meet with them here, in person. I explained I wanted to discuss engraining them in the culture of this town, and helping them find acceptance and peace in a way they could never have imagined. I had set up a meeting time at the coffee shop for twelve PM. An hour after closing.

The witching hour. The middle-of-the-day kind.

That's where I found myself, along with Gar and Jhamal, setting out a tray of specially baked cookies and muffins, as well as an assortment of teas and coffees. I couldn't tell Gar no when he had insisted on joining me. After all, he had put in most of the work to get everyone here. Plus, if I was going to convince a roomful of strangers that they could take the form of their Kin-Selves, it might be helpful to have an actual Totem Shifter in the room for demonstration purposes.

Cody had been adamant about coming along as well. He was convinced, now more than ever, that I might need saving if Mallis's witch attacked again. But I had assured him that his staying with my aunts was more important. I didn't like the idea of living them alone with Elion just yet, and thankfully he agreed.

"Are you sure about this?" said Jhamal, taking one of the muffins I had baked and stuffing it into his mouth whole.

"About what? And don't eat all of those! They're for our guests!"

He finished off the muffin and picked up one of the folded napkins to wipe his hands. "About telling everyone about what they could potentially do. I mean, have you even figured out the spell that can make turn them into Totems?"

"Of course I have." That was a lie. Granted, I was close, and I was pretty sure I would be able to do it, but still...

"Yeah right," said Gar. "I know when you're fibbing, sis. And even if you can do it, are you sure you should? I mean, what if some of them don't agree with the fight we are about to enter and want no part of it?"

"That's why I'm having them here," I replied. "I want to talk to them and figure out who's in and who's out before we do anything."

"Well, if it works, I think it will be cool," said Jhamal. "I've never met any Otherkin in real life, so I can't wait to chat with someone who really gets it."

I saw Gar wince in the slightest at this, but then almost as quickly he shrugged it off. We exchanged looks and his expression told me to drop it.

"And where are all of these people going to stay?" asked Gar.

"Well, we have some makeshift arrangements at the encampment, plus there are plenty of rooms available in all the bed and breakfasts around the area," I answered. The town should have been overrun with tourists this time of year— especially with the eclipse pending. The fact that there were "vacancy" signs dotting all the inns was troubling. Of course, if I didn't figure out a way to stop Mallis, Trinity's economy would be the last thing anyone would be worried about. "Plus, there will probably be plenty of people who'll get scared off, turn around, and head right back out of town." *I know I would.*

"Oh yeah, Esmay is dropping by as well," said Jhamal. "She said she has something for you."

Good. Esmay was the wife of Jhamal's aunt. She had been instrumental in saving my life, as well as Cody's, when Mallis had launched his first attacks on us. Her feisty nature and tongue as sharp as the rapier she always carried with her had made us friends almost immediately. Almost. Now, there were few other women I would want by my side when it came time to march into war.

There was no hiding my nerves. Speaking in front of crowds wasn't my thing. Granted, I had managed to convince a community of shifters to help us, but they had already been invested in Trinity Cove and wanted to put down roots here. Now, I would be trying to do the same thing but with strangers who had no discernible ties to the town. There was nothing to keep them from getting up and walking back out the same way they had come in, back into the night.

The chime of the door opening snapped me back to reality. I looked up to see a young woman in her early twenties walk into the shop. She was slight of build with straight dark hair that hung nearly to her waist. A baseball cap that read "FBI" was pulled tight over her head and it seemed to complement the loose-fitting jeans with the knees torn out and light blue t-shirt she wore.

"Hi, I'm Allie," I said, rushing over to greet her. "And this is my brother Gar and his boyfriend Jhamal."

"I'm Austin," she said, "or you may know me by my online handle of Red Foxy 101." I extended a hand and she shook it tentatively. Looking around she took in the space before turning back to me. "Am I the only one here?"

"So far. But I am hoping that changes," I responded. "Please, have a seat wherever you'd like and help yourself to some goodies. I baked them myself."

Austin eyed the muffins a little suspiciously before gingerly picking one up with a napkin and nibbling at it. She shrugged appreciatively and plopped down on the sofa across from the food. I finished putting out the plates before sitting in one of the chairs next to her.

"Thank you for coming," I said, trying to hide my nerves.

"Nothing to thank me for. I saw your post and answered

it. Your response made me curious enough to see for myself what is going on around here."

"What have you heard?" I asked.

She placed her muffin on the coffee table in front of her and looked up at me. "Just that this town is a hotbed of supernatural activity. That there is a vampire that has laid claim to it and the witches that live here are powerless to stop him."

"Well, I wouldn't say it's quite like that..." I began.

"Hey, my sister is far from powerless!" said Gar.

Before anyone could say another word, the door opened again. A man entered the shop wearing jeans and a blue and white striped t-shirt. He looked to be in his mid-thirties, and I was immediately struck by how handsome he was. Dark brown hair stylishly cut with just a few hints of gray sparkling throughout framed an angular face; a five o'clock shadow that looked more like an eleven o'clock one gave him the appearance of a man that had only recently accepted the fact that he was no longer seen as a hot twenty something. It was all set off by dazzling blue eyes that swept over everyone in the room, taking in the scenery in a glance.

"Hi, I'm Nate," he said, his voice pitched low, making every part of my body stand on edge and take notice.

I started towards him but was nearly knocked off my feet by Gar. "Hello and welcome! I'm Gar, the one who posted the messages on the forum. Did you find us okay...I mean, did you find your way here without any problems?" He had his hand out and was shaking Nate's furiously.

"Er, yeah, it was pretty straightforward. I've actually been through this town before, I live further up in the mountains toward Asheville."

"Oh wow...so beautiful...oops, I mean...Asheville.

Asheville is so beautiful. Not you…I mean…you're not *not* beautiful, but the mountains up there are."

My brother's rapidly spreading blush was making me laugh on the inside, but I didn't want him to scare off the man before we could find out what brought him in. I rushed over and introduced myself.

"I'm Allie, and we are very happy you have decided to join us. This is Austin, she just arrived as well. You've met my brother Gar, and this is Jhamal, his…"

"He's my boyfriend," said Gar, rushing over to take a startled Jhamal by the arm. "We're together."

"That's…nice. Good for you," Nate replied as he shook my hand and offered a magnificent smile.

"C'mon on in and help yourself to some coffee and snacks," I said gesturing toward the food laid out before us. "Take a seat wherever you'd like. We were just talking about what people outside the community of Trinity Cove are saying about our little town."

"Oh, you mean how this town is probably going to go the way of Sunnydale and be swallowed by a Hellmouth?" he answered. Austin gave a big smile and made a show of clapping her hands in approval at his remark.

"Eat your muffin," I told her before turning back to Nate. "Not going to happen. As long as I'm still standing, that is."

The door opened again and three more people walked in—two men and a woman, all young, barely out of their teens. It was now a quarter past the time we agreed to meet, so after asking them to come in I locked the door and placed a 'Closed' sign in the window. If anyone else showed, they'd have to announce their presence by knocking.

The young woman introduced herself as Lady and

motioned to her two friends. "That's Kinley and his brother Jase. They don't say much."

The two men barely acknowledged us and instead made for the two chairs at the far end of the shop close to the hallway that led to the bathrooms and plopped down. They were both tall and thin with bloodshot eyes, and I couldn't be certain if it was from too much time in front of the X-Box or too much time hitting certain herbs. My guess was the latter but I wasn't here to judge anyone.

Lady, on the other hand, definitely caught my attention. She was short and what my friend Hope would describe as "thick". To me, she looked like the majority of women I had been seeing around town lately. She was dressed in black leggings and a slouchy Under Armour sweatshirt that was two sizes too big for her frame. She wore a black beret from which a long braid of snow white hair flowed. She wore too much makeup around her eyes and her blood red lips automatically drew attention to her mouth. From the outside looking in, which was exactly what I was doing, I couldn't imagine what she and the two brothers had in common.

"So, your post said you could help us," Lady said, helping herself to two muffins before sitting down near the brothers. "How?"

"Well, first things first," I said. "Can everyone tell us what their Otherkin is?"

"You mean kintype," said Nate.

"Excuse me?" I said.

"It's called Kintype. We are all Otherkin, but each of our individual spiritual animals are called our Kintypes."

Pulling a chair away from one of the tables, I spun it around so that I could sit in the center of the room and addressed Nate. "I'm sorry. Thank you for correcting me. Would you be willing to share your Kintype with me?"

Nate swallowed hard and glanced around the room. All attention was focused on him—even the brothers' eyes were locked on him. He took a deep breath and nodded in my direction. "I'm a saber-toothed tiger."

I could see him practically holding his breath as he waited for the response. Not sure what he thought was going to happen but it probably wasn't the response he received from Austin.

"That is so friggin cool!" she exclaimed.

"Holy shit, she's right," added Lady. "And just when I thought you couldn't get any hotter." That made Nate blush and sink back into his chair.

"Good," I said. "That's good, because we can use all the muscle we can get. So who's next?"

"Okay, hold up," said Lady. "Why exactly are we doing this? You called us here but you haven't ponied up any info at all. How are you going to help us?"

I stood up and made myself sound as confident as possible. "I'm a witch, and this town has been invaded by an age-old vampire that is determined to return humanity to the dark ages. Literally. But I'm not going to allow that. He has an army of shifters on his side. I have a few. But I need to augment my troops with more shifters. Which would be you guys." I looked each of them in the eye before continuing. "I intend to cast a spell that will allow you to shift into your Kintype."

Now it was my turn to wait for the response with bated breath. I wasn't prepared for the response I received.

They laughed. Hard.

"I"m sorry," said Lady after she made a great show of trying to catch her breath and wipe tears from her eyes.

"You're going to cast a spell that will let us p-shift?" Again there was a round of laughter from the group.

"P-shift?" I asked.

"It stands for 'physical shift,'" said Austin. "It's not possible. We identify with our Kintype for deeply personal reasons, but we all know that p-shifting is a myth."

"Oh, really?" I said. "Jhamal, can you come here, please?"

He stepped out from the corner where he had been standing with Gar into the center of the room and stood facing everyone.

"Jhamal is Otherkin as well," I said. "Jhamal, what is your Kintype?"

"Lion," he replied smiling. Then, in the blink of an eye, he shifted into the large golden-maned lion that had recently wrecked such bloody havoc on a certain clan of shifters.

I reached up and rubbed his mane, smiling at the gaping mouths around me. "Who's laughing now?"

Chapter Seven

The initial shock gave way to a bevy of questions, all being thrown at me simultaneously. I held up both hands, urging silence. "Okay, calm down. I promise everyone will have the chance to ask all the questions they want, but one person at a time, please."

"How is this possible?" asked Nate. "We have all heard the stories of werewolves and shifters, but we aren't born into those families. Is he human?"

"Yes, he is human. Just like all of you. He is Otherkin… not shifter-born." I replied. "And his name is Jhamal." I saw Gar smile out of the corner of my eye and that made me smile. "As for how this is possible, it's magic. Real magic."

"So it's true then; you're the real thing," said Austin.

"I am indeed. I am a Reliquary Witch. I come from a long line of witches."

"So this," Lady said, gesturing at Jhamal, "is something you can do for all of us?"

"Well, that's the hope," I replied.

A quick silence descended before one of the brothers

found his voice. "You *hope*? Can't you just...do whatever you did with Jhamal?"

"I wasn't the one who did this. That was the result of another magic." Eyes that were just moments ago alive with hope and possibility were now downcast. "But that doesn't mean I can't still do it. I've studied the magic that created Jhamal's totem...the item that allows him to shift into his Kintype. I'm pretty sure I can recreate it."

The brothers glanced at one another and one of them leaned over to whisper in Lady's ear. She had moved to the couch to sit between the two of them. She nodded and looked at me. "So why did you bother getting us here? What's your endgame?"

"Her endgame was finding out what our Kintypes are so she can decide which of us are worthy of being able to p-shift. If she can even do it, that is." It was Nate who spoke up. His bright eyes were dark and murky now and focused on me with laser intent.

"Actually, I was the one who told her to get everyone talking by asking about your Kintypes," said Gar. "All of you here pretty much live online. The only people you talk to are fellow Otherkin and I'm willing to bet you've never met any of them in real life. Allie needs to know you can open up to one another and be trusted with this."

I nodded at Gar, once again thankful that my little brother was here. "Gar's right. I am not leading anyone on, or picking and choosing who will be able to do what. I just wanted everyone to be comfortable. I'm asking for your help in a war that could possibly get all of us killed. God knows the vampire that is after me certainly wants me dead. But I will gladly die if it means stopping him from taking over the world. And I stand a much better chance of stopping him if I have with more help."

That seemed to calm them down for the moment.

"So, this town really is infested with vamps and werewolves, huh?" said Austin. "What are they fighting over?"

I took a deep breath and dove into the retelling of what my family, friends, and I had recently faced. For the next hour I recounted all the horrors and threats, everything I had prayed to one day forget but deep down knew never would.

The room was so quiet you could literally hear a pin drop. Seriously, Jhamal dropped one of the toothpicks that held together a few wraps I had made to go with the appetizers, and everyone jumped at the sound.

"So this Mallis guy wants to recreate hell on earth, and he's out to kill you in order to make that happen?" said Austin. "And you're outnumbered and out-powered, right?"

"Outnumbered yes," I replied, "but not necessarily out-powered. And that's where everyone in this room comes into play."

"You need soldiers," said Nate dryly.

"Soldiers? No. That makes you sound expendable. I need people around me that care about doing the right thing as much as I do. People that want more for themselves and aren't going to stand around and let evil take over this world. Our world." I hoped my words were sinking in as I looked around at each of them. "We are building a community here...a community of those who are different, yet have a sense of belonging. I'll do this alone if I have to, but I'd certainly welcome any help I can get."

"Harpy eagle," said Austin.

"I'm sorry...what?" I replied.

"Me. My Kintype is a harpy eagle. I've always felt I was majestic and larger than any of the men around me that used to try and keep me in my place. Plus, I have great eyesight," she added, smiling.

One of the brothers—Kinley, I believe—stood up next. He looked around nervously. "I'm a..." he paused, his cheeks burning red, "I'm a honey badger."

To his credit, no one laughed. His brother, Jase, placed a hand on his shoulder proudly. "Nothing to be ashamed of, brother. That's one fucking vicious creature."

"And you?" I asked, looking at Jase.

He cleared his throat and proclaimed loudly, "Unicorn. A blue one, to be specific."

"A unicorn," said Austin. "Those don't exist."

"Can't help what I am," he said. "Ever since I was a child I was fascinated by...well, let's just say I'm also a closet Brony."

Good-natured laughter echoed around the room.

"What's a Brony?" I said.

"Oh Allie, you've so much to learn," said Gar. "A Brony is a man that is a fan of *My Little Pony.*"

"Oh. So that's a thing? Hey, you do you, my friend."

"So," said Nate, "that leaves you, Lady."

All eyes were on her and after what seemed an eternity of silence, she finally spoke up. "Me. I'm a minotaur."

"Wow," said Gar. "Kinda blows a lion and a saber-tooth out of the water." His smile was infectious, and everyone gave Lady an appreciative nod.

"Okay," said Jhamal, "then that gives us some serious firepower, right? A lion, a saber-tooth, a big-ass eagle, a unicorn, honey badger...and a minotaur. If Allie can make all this happen...we should be ready to do some serious ass-kicking, huh?"

"I don't know. I mean, I would hope so," I said, "but

Mallis has a lot of shifters at his disposal. And many of them are werewolves." I didn't want to touch his question about whether or not I could actually grant them shifting abilities.

"I might be able to help with that," said Nate. "I have an old friend that lives not far from me in the mountains. He's Otherkin as well. I think he might be able to help out. He's off the grid though, so I would have to go there in person to speak with him. But if you can make this work, he would be a powerful ally."

"What is his Kintype?" asked Gar.

"Grey Muzzle," said Nate. "He's a wolf...an older male wolf."

"We know someone as well," said Jase. "A friend of ours that...well, let's just say he could more than even the odds... if we can convince him to join."

The excitement I felt was palpable, but more than that, I was starting to feel something I hadn't for a while now: hope. Together, we could do this. Seeing the eagerness on their faces emboldened me.

"Austin," I said, "come here." I motioned for her to leave her seat and stand with me. The room went eerily quiet as she approached. "Do you have a piece of jewelry, something that you always wear and has great meaning to you?"

"Allie, what are you doing?" asked Gar, stepping forward. "You said you needed..."

"I know what I said Gar, but I got this."

I ignored the frown on his face as Austin removed a silver ring from her finger.

"But you said you needed our aunts' help to do this," Gar continued.

"Maybe. But I've been studying Jhamal's necklace, and I

can *read* the magic that is locked inside it. I know I can reproduce it." *Okay, maybe I'm...pretty sure I can reproduce it.*

But what would be the harm in at least trying? Everyone in this room had come because I had called out to them. They would stay if I could deliver on the unspoken promise I had made by having Jhamal shift in front of them. I could do this. I had to.

The ring was heavier than it looked—a sign that it was pure silver and not plated. That was a good thing, as I had discovered silver was one of the metals that most effectively conducted magic. Closing my fist around the band, I reached into it with my magic. I could feel the connection between the piece and Austin. There was deep attachment to it; someone very close to had given it to her. The connection was old, older than what it would be if it were from a lover. No, I was betting it was a parent, someone that had given great meaning to it, made it more than just a piece of jewelry.

I could work with that.

Basically, all I needed to do was combine a spell of revelation with an activation spell. At least, I *hoped* that was all I needed to do. I had studied Jhamal's necklace in great magical detail. The power that shaped it was very old and very strong. But deep down, it was a magic of calling, a magic that reached into the core of Jhamal's being and granted his spirit power and presence. It was similar to what I had done with Cody the first time I'd triggered his shift and gave him control of the wolf that lingered inside him.

But the difference there was Cody was born a shifter; the wolf was who he was. All I did was call to it and coax it out. These were humans. I had no idea what a dose of magic would do to them. How would animating their inner Othertype work when fused to the totem...in this case, the ring that Austin wore? The one thing I learned from studying Jhamal's necklace was that the magic was definitely in the totem; he couldn't shift without wearing it. That meant there was a flaw in the power...one that hopefully I could correct.

I cast doubt out of my mind and cleared my thoughts. Everything around me melted away until there was only one thing left for me to focus on: Austin's ring. My magic sang and whispered to me as I called it forth, pouring it into the ring and suffusing the metal with power.

At the same time, I drew up what I hoped was just the right spell to call out an inner Kintype. In studying Jhamal's necklace, I realized that it was tied to a type of revelation spell. That was what allowed him to become who he felt he was on the inside. There had been other trace elements of magic as well...most of which I didn't recognize, but I was pretty sure I had the basics needed to pull this off.

When I had triggered Cody's transformation and given him control of it, I had pretty much done the same thing. As a Reliquary witch, I had the raw power inside me to pretty much do whatever I wanted. But instinct told me this required more finesse than using a sledgehammer. I couldn't just force the power to transform it into being...I had to coax it out willingly.

Unlike with Cody, there was nothing that felt even remotely supernatural dwelling within Austin. I probed her with magic, yet all I felt was her humanity. This was going to be more difficult than I thought. There was nothing to work with, nothing to shape. Maybe I had made a mistake? But Jhamal was human as well...I was sure of that. Why was he able to shift? It was more than just the necklace, the totem, that created him. I had to look deeper inside of Austin if I was going to make this work.

The good news was that I had never felt more in tune with my power; it was practically alive and flowing within me. I could see, hear, taste, feel and smell everything around me. The power sang to me, reassuring me with its presence; no matter what happened, it would always be here for me, it whispered.

That was it. That was the key. My magic was...who I was. I created it and summoned it when I needed to, and that was what I needed to do for the Otherkin. The wolf that lived inside Cody was a part of him, but unlike the Otherkin, it was a part of him that he did not know existed.

He hadn't created it.

Again I needed to go deeper with my magic if I was going to make this work. I relaxed, sinking deeper into my mind. I let my head drop, resting my chin on my chest. My magic anchored me as my body rose off the floor and I crossed my legs underneath me, floating a few feet above the floor. The ring burned in my hand as I opened my fist, letting it rest in my palm. This time, I didn't concentrate solely on the ring, but on Austin as well. I reached deep into the young woman's mind, burning past her conscious thoughts and fears, and sought out her true core.

The part of her that had never been swayed by another living soul...that part of her being that was her refuge from all the insults and jibes that had been cast her way by classmates, friends, and even family. There, beneath the turmoil of self-doubt and anger, I saw a light flickering. It was the untouched truth of who she knew herself to be. I couldn't make out anything within the light, but I could hear in the distance the faint call of a bird.

An eagle, to be exact.

This was the self she had created long ago on a subconscious level. It wasn't until later that she'd given it a name and a shape. This was primal Austin, and I reached out with my magic with all the strength I could.

It was like pouring gasoline on a match; the small spark blazed to an inferno within her.

I heard her physical self scream out in response and I sensed her fall to the floor. Too late to stop it now, though. The ring burned white-hot in my hand, and looking over at Austin, I commanded the spell of revelation to fully awaken who she was. At the same time, I threw the silver band at her. It flew through the air in a blue streak of power, slipped itself back onto her finger, its burning glow spreading to encompass her entire body.

Austin screamed, but I couldn't tell if it was in pain or ecstasy. Either way, I threw more magic at her, practically willing the spell to work. She looked over at me, her face awash in mystical energy, and I could have sworn I saw her smile.

Then she arched her back, throwing her face to the ceiling as she lifted her arms from her side. Then, with a blinding flash of light, accompanied by a small clap of thunder, she was gone.

Chapter Eight

Everyone shook their heads, clearing away the leftover buzzing created by the thunder.

To my eyes, the room was alive with magic...my magic. It filled the space, flowing into and around everyone, licking at them like flames leaping up from a newly-lit campfire.

I smiled as I heard everyone gasp. Auston was indeed gone, and in her place stood a magnificent creature.

A harpy eagle.

I knew what an eagle looked like, but I had never seen a harpy eagle before. The form Austin had taken was that of a large raptor, standing nearly five feet in height, with brilliant sapphire blue and black plumage. She looked like an American eagle, but with a large double-crested crown of feathers on her head that gave her a horned appearance. A white underbelly contrasted sharply with the bright blue wing feathers and the shimmering plumage that ran down her back. Her eyes were pitch black and shone fiercely in the dim light, peeking out from a white and gray face that was dominated by a large, gracefully curving beak. She stood on strong, stout legs that ended in inch-long, curved talons.

Shock seemed to momentarily wipe away everyone's ability to speak. Everyone except Austin, that was. She lifted her beak to the ceiling and let loose a wailing cry that pierced my eardrums. I joined everybody else in the room in covering my ears just as she spread her wings, revealing an unbelievable wingspan that easily exceeded twelve feet. One flap caused the small table that held the refreshments to flip over, spilling finger food and coffee cups everywhere.

My new group of friends scattered as she tried to flap in order to gain air. Chairs flew across the room, and the two brothers dove to protect Lady as all three were thrown against the back wall from the updraft Austin was creating. I had to put a stop to this. The coffee shop wasn't built to withstand the force of the wind shear she could generate.

"Austin!" I screamed over the din. Between the roar of the wind her flapping wings generated and the ghostly wail of her cry, I wasn't sure my voice could even reach her. "Austin, stop! You're going to hurt someone!" Actually, I was afraid she was about to *kill* someone if I didn't get this under control.

I grabbed at the ambient magic I could see swirling around the room and gathered it around Austin in glowing bands that closed over her feathery form, pinning her massive wings at her side. This made her screech even louder, but at least it allowed me to approach her without fear of being beaten unconscious, or worse.

"It's okay," I said, reaching out to stroke her with my hand and my magic. "You're okay...I can't imagine what this must feel like for you, but underneath all of the feathers and new senses that you are now experiencing the world through, remember who you are."

Heat rolled off of her in waves. It was new magic and it was looking for place to go. I gathered it up and bent it gently, coaxing it to flow back into Austin, helping her to find herself. What if this was too much for her? What if my magic had not only warped her physical self but had trapped her mind as well? What if she no longer had a mind and had become all fury and raptor? *Damnit*! Why hadn't I waited until my aunts were around to try this?

No. No time for self doubt now. I made the decision to do this, so that meant I had to be the one to fix it. But the problem was, I couldn't see where anything had gone wrong. To my mind's eye, Austin was awash with magic... her shifter form was pure mystical energy through and through. It looked just like Jhamal's did; all glowing magical goodness.

"Austin," I continued, "this is who you were meant to be. You are free now." Her eyes, dark and hard, looked at me. Then, they softened, and somewhere within their limitless black depths, I saw a spark of recognition. "Yes. Yes, that's it. It's me...Allie. You're surrounded by all of your new friends, and we are all so happy to meet the real you at last. Can you hear me?"

Her screeching had stopped and her head cocked to one side as those black eyes took in the figures around the room.

"I'm going to release you now...I need you to stay calm and focused, okay?"

I slowly broke the magical bands that held her. Gar made a move to step forward but I motioned him back. There was only one binding left, and when I mentally dissolved it, Austin was completely free. Her feathers ruffled slightly but she remained calm, her eyes focused on me as I once again reached up to stroke her head.

"Very good, Austin," I said softly. "Now. I need you to

feel deep inside of yourself and find that trigger. The one that is tied to your human form. I need you to find it and switch it on…be human again. I can't help you with this part…" I slowly backed away, calling my magic with me, drawing all of it back inside me and away from our newest shifter.

Other than the heavy breathing around me, the room was silent. Austin regarded us all indifferently, her head moving quickly from side to side as she took in all four corners of the space. Slowly, she once again spread her wings, and I called up a small ball of magic and held it at the ready just in case I needed to take her down before she could do any real damage. But instead of whipping the air inside the shop into a frenzy, she simply held her wings open and aloft. Then, in the blink of an eye and another blast of white light, the eagle was gone and the woman returned.

Austin collapsed, dropping onto her knees, a puppet with cut strings. Everyone else was too stunned to move, but I rushed to her side, placing one hand on her back as I knelt beside her.

"Hey, it's okay. What do you need?" I asked.

"Water," she managed. "I'm…so thirsty."

Gar vanished behind the counter display and returned with a bottle of water that Austin proceeded to down in a few giant gulps.

"Austin!" said Lady coming to stand next to us. "What was it like?"

"It was incredible…I'm not even sure I can describe it. I was me…but at the same time I wasn't. At first I was completely freaked out. My senses…I can't even describe how the world looked and sounded to me. I didn't know how to process anything. But then, I heard Allie's voice and felt…I don't know, something reaching into me and soothing me. It allowed me to gain the control I needed. Holy shit, you guys! I can't wait for you to experience it!"

Lady turned to me, tears in her eyes. "You did it. You freaking did it!" She threw herself against me, wrapping me in a bear hug before turning to everyone else. "So. Who's next?"

Chapter Nine

Exhaustion hit me like the proverbial ton of bricks. Aunt Vivian and Aunt Lena read me the riot act when I told them what I had done.

"Allie, what were you thinking?" said Aunt Vivian. "You could have been killed trying a spell like that! Or just as bad, you could have killed those people!"

"But Aunt Vivian I..."

"No buts, young lady!" chimed in Aunt Lena. "What you did was exceptionally reckless. To say nothing of the fact that you disobeyed your Aunt and I."

There was no arguing that point. Granted, I'd done what I had to do, but they were right. It had been dangerous. But at least I'd been able to minimize the danger primarily to myself.

"You have no idea what could have happened, Allie," said Aunt Vivian. "What if the spell had went off in a weird direction and turned them into raving lunatics? What if you had turned them into...animals, or whatever, and they had no recollection of their human selves at all? No way of getting back? You could have driven them mad, Allie!"

Aunt Lena took a deep breath. She could sense that I was a girl on the verge at this point. "Allie," she said in a softer voice, "you are a Reliquary. You have a responsibility. You are too important in this fight to go off and risk your life like that."

"I know you are coming from a place of love," I said, "and I truly respect you both. But love is the very reason I did what I did. I knew there were risks—and I couldn't stand the thought of the two of your taking those risks. I've seen too many people die in this fight already. I couldn't willingly place my family in harm's way; I had to at least make the attempt to cast that spell."

"What about your brother?" said Aunt Vivian. "What about Gar? You would risk his life? He is completely unprepared to face the forces you called upon!"

"Jhamal was there!" I said. "He would never let anything happen to Gar. You know that. Besides, I needed Gar to be there as much as he needed to be there. I can't explain it, but keeping him chained here in the house to protect him was having the exact opposite effect on him. At least having him at my side, I could keep an eye on him."

This quieted them both for a second. I was too tired to argue and plopped down on the sofa in the living room.

"Speaking of, where is he?" said Aunt Lena.

"He went with Jhamal back to his aunt's house. I offered to send Jhamal with Nate up to the mountains to help convince a friend of Nate's—another Otherkin—to join us, but Nate declined. He thinks he will stand a better chance of getting his friend's help if he's alone. They are dropping Gar off here on their way up to the mountains."

"And Nate would be…?" inquired Aunt Vivian.

"He's a saber-toothed tiger. A big one. No way Mallis will be expecting that."

Aunt Lena took a seat next to me on the couch. "Allie, you are doing too much. I can see the exhaustion in you."

I shook my head. "You just said I have a responsibility. What I am—even though I never asked for it—means that I don't get the luxury of saying something is too much. Like it or not, my job is to do whatever it takes to end this war before it starts. If I'm not already too late, that is." Despite my words, I could feel the need for sleep pulling at me, and for a moment I sensed the world closing in around me. My bed was calling and I needed to get there before I passed out in front of my aunts.

The room spun when I tried to get to my feet and I hastily sat back down, holding my now throbbing head.

"Allie," said Aunt Vivian, "are you alright? What's wrong?"

"Nothing. I'm okay…I think I just overdid it with the magic. I guess I do have my limits, after all."

But I knew this was not simple exhaustion. I felt like I had when I was on the deck with Aunt Lena and collapsed. Jesus, not again. I could feel the pull of the darkness, but this time, I was ready. I called on my magic and threw it out around me. My aunts must have sensed what I was doing because I felt the gentle hum of their own power build up and flow protectively around me as well.

It wasn't enough, and I could feel myself sliding towards the darkness. It clawed at my consciousness, eating away at my rational thoughts until I could once again feel myself dissolving into that terrifying nothingness. I lapsed back on the couch, ready to surrender to whatever hell would be waiting for me this time, when it suddenly passed.

As quickly as it hit me, it was gone.

"Was that...?" began Aunt Lena.

"Yes," I croaked, "the same attack from earlier. But it stopped this time."

"Are you okay?" Aunt Vivian asked.

"I...I need some water, please. I feel very weak."

"Weak" was an understatement. A really feisty kitten could have taken me out at this point. The magic I had thrown out had dissipated, and try as I might, I couldn't call anymore up. I couldn't sense my aunts' magics either. What the hell was going on with me?

I managed to sit up enough to take the cup of water Aunt Lena offered me in shaky hands. My throat felt like it was on fire and the water was a brief, cool salve that cleared my head and put out the fire that smoldered inside me.

"You're burning up, Allie," said Aunt Lena, placing a hand on my forehead.

"It's the same attack she suffered before," said Aunt Vivian. She was standing as she spoke, and abruptly she turned her back to me, facing the large triple windows that opened up to the front lawn.

She made grand sweeping gestures in the air, her arms moving in quick, intricate bursts. Her fingers were intertwined and her hands danced in a complex rhythmical movement that told me she was casting a very specific spell.

"Do you have it?" asked Aunt Lena.

"No. It's too slippery...deliberately dodging me," Aunt Vivian replied.

Instantly, Aunt Lena was on her feet. Her movements began to mirror her sister's as they began an intricate dance of hand and finger movements. The air around them hummed with power as they harnessed magic and focused it toward a common goal.

"There!" said Aunt Lena. Simultaneously, they clasped

their hands together, pointer fingers extended and flush against one another as they forcefully raised their arms skyward, aiming at something I could not see. Then they lowered their arms and pulled their hands in close to their midsections before turning to face one another.

"Well done, sister," said Aunt Vivian.

"What happened?" I asked. "What was well done?"

"Allie, how do you feel?" asked Aunt Lena.

"Like…" I almost said "shit," but was stopped not only by remembering how my aunts felt about swearing, but also because I no longer felt like shit. "I actually feel better." I sat up and looked around. No nausea, no vertigo. "Wow…I feel like nothing happened to me. What did you do?"

"Well, we divided a way to tap into the magical remnants of the signature that attacked you earlier," said Aunt Vivian. "Once Elion told us the attack was mystical in nature, then we knew there had to be a mystical defense."

"We made a subtle alteration to the wards around the house," added Aunt Lena, "so that we would be tipped off in the event that whatever attacked you tried again. And when that happened, we were ready with a counterattack."

"One that not only repelled that disgusting blood magic spell, but also allowed us to see the origin of the magic."

I bolted to my feet, beaming at my aunt. "You mean, you saw the witch that did this?"

"No. Unfortunately she remained hidden, bouncing the spell off of a refractor," said Aunt Vivian.

"A refractor? What's that?" I offered the couch to my aunts. The magic they used looked like it had wiped them out.

"Just what it sounds like," said Aunt Lena. "It's an artifact that a witch has familiarized herself with. She can then use it as a remote lens, if you will, to focus her spells. Typically it's used for scrying…a mirror or other object that a witch can leave in a premise she no longer inhabits, but may still want to keep an eye on from afar."

"Kind of the way a spy uses bugs…I get it," I said.

"Exactly," continued Aunt Lena, "but in this case, the witch was using the refractor to bounce her spell before it struck at you. Very clever. Her way of making sure we could not track her location."

"Very clever indeed," said Aunt Vivian, "but maybe not clever enough. While I could not see the witch herself, I did get the location of the artifact she was using to transmit her magic."

"Excellent," I said. "Point me in the direction. Maybe there will be some clues left behind that tell us where she is."

"You're not going by yourself," said Aunt Vivian. "So you can put that thought right out of your head."

"But Aunt Vivian, neither of you look like you're in any shape to leave the house. And like I said, I'm…"

"Girl, have you not heard a word we have been saying," said Aunt Lena. Her hand reached out to grasp mine and her warm, soft eyes searched my face. "Haven't you realized yet that we are all stronger together?"

Before I could say anything, the front door opened. Cody and Elion strode through, both stopping just inside the doorway, staring at the three of us.

"What's going on? What's wrong," said Cody. He moved immediately to stand by my side. Elion remained where he was, spine stiff, his head cocked at a slight angle as if he was listening for something.

"Nothing," I said, shrinking back slightly. "Where have you two been?" I noticed for the first time that it was almost dawn.

"I am still healing," said Elion. "My injuries were a little deeper than I thought. I needed blood."

My eyes darted questioningly from him to Cody.

"Don't worry," said the vampire. "Your boyfriend was kind enough to...escort me on my hunt."

"He only took down a deer," said Cody. "An older one, that he somehow knew had no fawns...or mates."

"So you can feed on animals," I said. "Why not do that all the time?"

Elion shrugged. "It's not the same. But in a crunch... any port in a storm will do." He shrugged his shoulders in a way that almost made him seem human.

"Hey, forget about him," said Cody, "what's going on here?"

"Allie was attacked again," said Aunt Vivian, "by the same dark magic that almost felled her before. But my sister and I were ready this time. We tracked the magic to an artifact...and now Allie wants to run off and investigate it on her own."

My ears and face burned as I felt Cody's eyes track over to me.

"Nope, not a chance," he said. "While I do think we need to investigate, you won't be going alone. When do we leave?"

I took his hand and leaned into him. As ready as my world was feeling right then, it just became a little more solid.

Aunt Lean smiled approvingly. "If you wait until the evening, you can be a little more rested and you will be able to take Elion along with you. A vampire's senses may come in handy."

I was about to protest, but remembered that I had indeed been up all night and had also expended a considerable amount of magic. Rest and food sounded like heaven right about now.

"Fine," I said. "Plus, it will give me time to introduce you to a few more friends that we now have on our side."

"Where exactly are we going?" asked Cody.

"I tracked the spell to what looked like an old farmhouse on the outskirts of the city," said Aunt Vivian. "I can whip up a beacon spell that will draw you right to it when it's time to go."

I nodded and thanked her. I looked at Cody and could tell we were thinking the same thing: trap. Not that it mattered. I didn't care who or what was waiting for me; it was time to strike hard and fast.

Chapter Ten

The day passed wonderfully uneventfully. Cody curled up next to me and I was out before I could even appreciate the warmth of his body pressed against mine. No dreams, nothing to disturb me, just rest. I woke up many hours later in the same position I had fallen asleep in. I tossed aside the light comforter Cody had draped over me and stretched. Sleep had done me a world of good, and I could once again feel the reassuring buzz of my magic.

"Welcome back," I whispered to it, "you scared me for a minute there."

Through the closed bedroom door I could hear a cacophony of voices rising and falling throughout the house. I slipped on a pair of bath shoes, I hurried out to see what was going on.

The kitchen and living room were awash with people. Looking around, I made out many of the people I had met last night, including Austin, Lady and the two brothers. I could hear Gar's voice coming from outside on the deck. The double doors leading from the kitchen to the outdoors were thrown open, letting the cool dusk breeze ventilate the space.

"Austin, Lady…what's going on?" I asked.

"Ah, there she is," said Austin, coming over to throw her arm around me shoulder. "Our hero!" I blushed, and that made Austin laugh heartily before playfully jabbing at my arm. "Garland invited us all over."

"Oh, really?" I said, looking around for my brother. A moment later, he entered from the basement stairs, carrying a large pack of bottled water. Smiling, he brushed past me and plunked it down on the large center island in the kitchen.

"Oh hey, you're up," he said. "I tried to keep it quiet but it was getting harder and harder to do that."

"I can see that. Mind telling me what everyone is doing here?"

"This? Oh, it was my doing." Gar made his way out of the kitchen and stood next to me.

"And by 'your doing' you mean…?"

He gave me that sheepish look he hadn't used since we were kids. He ran one hand through his hair, his eyes darting about the room. "Well, I kind of invited all of the Otherkind we met to…stay here."

"You *what*? Gar, what were you…I mean…" I look around at the crowd assembled in our home. "Gar, I'm sure you had nothing but the best of intentions, but…I mean, physically where are we putting everyone? How is this going to work from just a space standpoint?"

"It's not going to be forever Allie." He took me by my elbow and led me away from the murmuring crowd, outside onto the deck. We sat on the couch at the far end, out of earshot. "Look, this is kind of our fault." I gave him a side eye and he held up one hand to stop me before I could speak. "I mean, think about it, they wouldn't even be here if we hadn't put out the call for help." That shut me up. "They are helping us, Allie. It's the least we can do."

I smiled and ruffled my little brother's hair. "But where are they going to sleep, Gar? I mean, this place is big and all, but last I checked there wasn't another hidden floor with an extra ten bedrooms."

"Well, technically that isn't exactly true…" Aunt Lena walked out onto the deck towards us.

"Aunt Lena," I said, "you heard that?"

"I may be getting older, but luckily, my senses aren't. Not yet anyway." She gave a hearty little laugh and motioned for me to scoot over and make room for her. She turned to face me. "What your brother did was admirable, Allie. Did you even consider where all of your new friends would stay?"

"Well…I thought maybe the shifter community would take them in until…"

"Until when?" she interjected. "Until after the war is over, when who knows how many of them and us will still be standing? Allie, all these people left their lives to follow you. You asked them here. What Gar did was the right thing."

"I guess I just didn't think it was cool to ask them to give up their homes and fight for us, but then tell them they have to live in a commune outside of the town they're fighting for until all of this is over," Gar added. "The shifters living up there are one thing. They made the decision to move there. The Otherkind did not."

"No, of course. You're absolutely right," I said. "But that brings us back to your cryptic statement, Aunt Lena."

"Yes," she began, "well, this house is a lot more than meets the eye, my dear."

"Oh is it a Decepticon or an Autobot?" Gar chimed in. The glare I gave him only made him shrug.

"Ummm, I'm not sure what you mean by that," said Aunt Lena, "but I'm just going to ignore it. This house is built on a very specific type of Ley line, the innate power that runs throughout the bedrock of this town. In our case, the house is constructed over the conflux of mystical power that warps spatial configurations."

"Okay that sounds like something Lieutenant Data would say," said Gar.

I had to agree. I was lost. "What does that mean?"

"It means that we have more room than you would think," said Aunt Lena with a wink. "Tell me, have you checked out the attic?"

"We don't have an attic," I answered.

"Oh really?" she said, arching both eyebrows in a truly comic fashion. "You mean you have never wondered what that pulldown door in the ceiling outside of our study is?"

Gar and I looked at one another questioningly. We had explored every inch of the house over the years; there was absolutely no way we would have missed seeing an attic door.

"Why don't you go check?" said Aunt Lena. "I'm going to make myself some tea." With that, she stood and started back towards the kitchen.

Gar and I followed, but then made our way through the crowd of people to the stairs that led up to the loft and our aunts' study. There, just before the closed door that led into their most private of spaces, was an attic door cut into the ceiling from which a white cord dangled. How had we never noticed it before? Grabbing the large wooden handle that was tied to the end of the cord, I gave it a pull. The door dropped down smoothly, and a wooden ladder that was

The Return of the Witch

folded in on itself sat attached to the inside of the trap door. We unfolded it so that the ladder was planted on the carpeted hallway, inviting us up into the—until now—hidden space.

Gar didn't hesitate; he brushed past me and climbed into the attic. For once I wasn't worried because I knew that our aunt would not have sent us to explore a space that could present a danger to either of us.

"Oh, wow!" said Gar stopping halfway up the ladder. Then he quickly finished his climb, hauling himself out of my view.

"What is it?" I called up after him. "What do you see?"

"Allie, get up here. You have to see it for yourself."

I followed my brother up the ladder and stuck my head into the space that before now didn't exist. Well not to us, anyway. What I saw defied description. It shouldn't have been there, but somehow, there was what appeared to be another full floor of living space sprawling out before us.

"Gar...how can this be?"

He was too busy studying the space around us to answer. Making the turn from the attic entrance revealed a large, open living area comprised of another kitchen and comfortably-appointed living room, complete with television, beautiful furnishings, a full floor-to-ceiling bookcase and wonderful floor lamps flooding the room with an abundance of light.

Branching off from the great room were a series of hallways that led to closed doors. I followed one of the halls and opened the door to see what was behind it. It led into a very comfortable bedroom, complete with a full en-suite bath. How was this possible?

Walking back up the hall, I ran into Gar coming from one of the hallways that had split off opposite the one I had taken. "Bedroom?" He only nodded before shaking his head in amazement.

"This is crazy, sis!"

I could only agree as we walked back into the great room. Looking around, I counted ten hallways branching off of it. We would definitely have more than enough room for everyone now. But I was still marveling at how this was even possible. I had started to think that I was the shit with magic, but maybe there was still a ton I needed to learn, because clearly the laws of physics were not at play when it came to this house.

We both went back downstairs and smiled at the knowing looks the aunts gave us. The considerable space up there solved the issue of where everyone would sleep. But that wasn't the only problem facing us right now.

"Everyone, if I can have your attention for a minute…" I said, making my way to center of the living room. "First, thank you for all agreeing to fight with me and my family in this war."

"No," said Lady stepping forward, "it's we who thank you, Allie. You've given us something that is beyond any hopes or dreams that any of us could have fathomed. I know what is being asked of us…and I for one am ready to make the ultimate sacrifice if need be. Just having a moment of true realization and experiencing my true self… it was beyond what I could have ever imagined. And definitely worth fighting to the death over."

A mummer of agreement passed through my new friends and all of them were nodding in agreement. It was almost too much for me, but I blinked back my tears and smiled back at everyone.

"We're going to do this," I said. "I don't care what gets thrown at us…we're not losing. We can't. Tonight, I want everyone to settle in." I saw Gar's body stiffen out of the corner of my eye.

"We're going with you," he said before I could stop him.

"What? Where are you going?" said Austin.

"She's going after someone who's been using magic to attack her lately. Most likely the witch consort of the vampire that is trying to kill her," replied Gar, his eyes burning into me.

"I'm not going to confront anyone," I say. "The witch is using some sort of artifact to bounce her spells off. If I can find it and take it out, it will mean she has to attack me more directly. Taking away her ability to launch sneak attacks levels the playing field."

"You're not going alone," said Austin. "That's what we are here for, right? To provide backup and muscle?"

"Yes," I admitted. "But tonight is not the night. You've only just been reborn as a shifter. I would rather you get little more used to your new forms. None of you are battle-tested and tonight is not the night to try out your new powers." All eyes were on me and I could feel them weighing my words. "Plus, there is no reason to think tonight will be anything other than an ordinary snatch and grab. Also, I think you will all be more effective with the element of surprise on your side."

"But you can't go out alone, Allie. I thought that was the plan; to have the Totem Shifters here as backup?" said Gar.

"Right now Mallis has no idea you all even exist. We don't want to ruin that by needlessly revealing your presence tonight."

"And she won't be alone," came a voice from the stairwell. Elion entered the room, effortlessly gliding between bodies until he reached my side. He tilted his head to one side, surveying my new friends. "Very interesting."

"We are going as backup as well." It was Cody this time. He walked in through the front door and tossed his keys onto the entry table. "I picked up a friend."

Esmee entered the room behind him. Her hair was pulled back into a high ponytail, and I could see the hilt of her silver rapier peeking above the collar of her black leather jacket. "Hello, Allie. So, you thought you were the only one having fun tonight?"

I glanced at Cody, not bothering to hide my annoyance. "Cody, it was just supposed to be the three of us. I don't want anyone put in danger that doesn't need to be."

"You aren't the only one that has been attacked, Allie," said Esmee. "We've been through this. I still owe that vampire bastard and his she-wolf a beatdown. Besides, if something happens to you, we are all royally fucked. So yeah. I got your back no matter where you're going."

Warmth spread throughout my body. The kind of genuine warmth that only true friendship and love can bring. I really was feeling like the luckiest witch in the world right then.

"Okay then," I said. "That settles it. Cody, Esmee, Elion and I will go to try to find out what the witch is using to cloak herself with. The rest of you settle in and get some rest. We only have a few days left until the eclipse so I have a feeling things are about to ramp up around here."

"What about me?" asked Gar. "Jhamal and I can help as well."

"No, you stay here. I would rather Jhamal be here to help the new Totem shifters acclimate to their new abilities." His shoulders slumped and he cast his eyes down at his shoes. "Besides, what I'm about to do is a piece of cake. You have a much harder job tonight."

"What's that?" he asked suspiciously.

"You get to settle all the fights between everyone when they start picking their rooms upstairs." Despite himself, he laughed at the thought, his face lighting up at the possibilities.

Turning to my aunts I hugged them both. Aunt Lena gave me a silver strand with a blue crystal attached to the end of it.

"This will lead you to the spot we saw," she said. "Be careful, Allie. This witch is nobody to play around with."

I looked over at Cody and nodded. "Neither are we, Aunt Lena. Neither are we."

With that, we left the house and piled into Esmee's Navigator. It was time to stop playing defense and ram this ball down someone's throat.

As soon as we piled into the car, the crystal Aunt Lena had given me fired to life. It burned brightly in the darkness and tugged at its chain, pulling up and outward until the tether was taut and the crystal pointed to the right.

"I guess we go right," I said. Esmee eased the big SUV out of the drive and headed in the direction the crystal indicated.

"Cool trick," she said glancing at the glowing gem. "Would make a hell of a replacement for my maps navigation system."

"It's a scrying crystal," I said. "They are meant to seek out and locate whatever they are enchanted to find. In this case, my aunts commanded it to lock onto the signature given off by the artifact the witch was using to attack me."

"Oh," said Esmee, "so what you're saying is it won't help me to find a Starbucks if I'm in a new town, huh?"

I couldn't help but laugh, and it seemed to release all the tension in the air. I turned in my seat enough to catch a glimpse of Cody in the backseat. "You boys good back there?"

Cody snorted in response. "Just peachy." He was staring at Elion, who was sitting ramrod still next to him.

"Okay, if no one else will, I'll say it's time we address the…er…wolf in the room," said Esmee. "What is going on between you two?" She glanced into the rearview window, her eyes darting from Cody to Elion.

"It's a supernatural thing," said Elion. "Wolves and vampires are not created to be…equals."

"The fuck is that supposed to mean?" said Cody heatedly.

"It's the truth," said Elion. "Your kind was created with the express purpose of serving my kind. You were our daytime watchdogs. No offense, of course."

"Oh, I don't know," I chimed in, trying to defuse the situation. "Sounded pretty offensive to me."

"Agreed," added Esmee with just a touch of annoyance creeping into her voice. "Play nice back there. Isla will kill me if I get claw marks in the leather."

Cody snorted. "It's something instinctive isn't it?" He directed this at Elion. "I don't know why, but from the moment I laid eyes on you, I not only didn't trust you, but I didn't like you either."

"There was a time," said Elion, "when you would have given your front paws to protect my kind. But that was many, many of your generations ago." He sound almost remorseful.

"So what, you miss having your slaves?" said Cody. His voice was raw with emotion that I had never heard from him before.

"What? Not at all," replied Elion. "I remember when the first wolves were created. How your ancestors fought against the sting of the vampires' silver-laced whips until you were finally beaten into submission. I watched as the light of defiance was smothered out of you. I saw you become…domesticated.

"The truth was that we didn't really need you. At the time, there was civil war brewing among the ranks of the vampire elite. Some of our kind had splintered off to form new clans of our own, away from the Mallises of our world. Yes, we may have done some pretty terrible things, but believe it or not, not all of us wanted to pillage the land and feed on every human we came across. Some of us simply wanted to be left alone. We were powerful enough that we had no need to fear the humans that were foolish enough to hunt us. However, the witches…" I could feel him glance at me, "that was a different story. But we knew that they would not hunt us as long as we left them alone. Back then, they didn't go around looking to be the defenders of mankind. They kept to themselves and minded their business.

"It was Mallis and his cabal that started the war with the witches. He wanted their power for his own. When he could not replicate the power, he discovered a way to tether male witches to their female counterparts and siphon their power for his own vile uses. He started the war that resulted in the birth of the wolves. Creatures that were designed to protect us from witches and…" His voice trailed off and he turned his head to stare out the window.

"And what?" I said. "You've said this much, might as well get it all out in the open."

He turned to face Cody and I could tell he was measuring his words carefully. "Your kind was not originally created to be our daytime bodyguards. You were created to hunt witches. Sniff them out, bring them to us…or kill them."

"What?" exclaimed Cody. "That's a lie!"

"Why would I lie about such a thing? I was there…I know what your original purpose was."

"So you're saying the werewolves were created to… kidnap witches for Mallis?" I asked.

"Kidnap…among other things," said Elion.

The silence that descended in the car was more than oppressive. I wanted to do something, to yell at Elion, to call him a liar and let him know that what he was saying didn't make sense. But part of me, somewhere in the back of my mind, was replaying the incident when I was snatched out of my body and cast into the blackness. The blackness where Cody's wolf was prowling.

"She knows," said Elion nodding in my direction. "She feels it. Probably always has. Haven't you ever wondered why the two of you are so drawn to one another? I bet it happened after he changed, didn't it? He could smell you long before he could put it into words what you were."

"Shut the fuck up!" yelled Cody. "You're a lying piece of shit, you know that?"

Elion didn't answer, but instead returned to looking out the window.

"Think about it," he finally said. "Mallis is so ancient that even the sun may not fully destroy him. Do you really think he needs protection from anything? He only covets more power…to use in his own dark, twisted ways. Your kind is the means for him to achieve that power."

Cody opened his mouth to respond but was cut off by Esmee. "Hey guys, does this road seem familiar to anyone?"

I had been so wrapped up in the conversation that I hadn't been paying attention to where we were going. The scrying crystal I held was pulling violently in my hand. The gem was flashing and sparking rapidly, trembling in midair as it struggled against the silver leash. Wherever we were going, it was very nearby.

I peered at the road we had turned down. To be honest, it looked like almost every other side road in Trinity Cove: unpaved and overgrown to either side with tall populars that reached across the road to touch branches. But Esmee was right, this did look familiar.

Then it hit me, and I struggled to hold back the bile that threatened to fill my throat.

"Hey," said Cody, "isn't this...?"

"Yes," I said. "The driveway that leads to Dr. Garner's house." *Or what was left of it.*

"Yes, that's it," said Esmee. "Isla and I came out here when we first moved to Trinity. There was nothing left of her aunt's farmhouse. We've never been back here since. But how do you know the house?"

"It's a long story," I said. "This is where Cody's father used to bring him for his medical care as a child."

"What? But like Isla, her aunt was a veterinarian, not a pediatrician...oh. I see." To her credit, if she was shocked, she didn't let on.

"Esmee, hold up, let's not get too close. Just in case," said Cody.

Esmee nodded and eased the car into the tall grass that made up the shoulder of the driveway. Placing the car in park, we all climbed out and surveyed the surroundings.

"I don't smell anything," said Cody.

"Nor do I," added Elion.

"That doesn't mean we're alone," said Esmee, drawing her rapier and holding it in front of her as we advanced.

"No need for magic to light the way this time," said Cody glancing skyward. I nodded.

Full moon tonight.

Even though considerable time had passed since the fire, I could still make out the smell of burning embers as we neared the ruins. The old house had once served as the community veterinary service and the personal abode of a highly respected member of our little society. The smells also brought back the memory of bloodshed and great violence. I tried to block out the picture of Dr. Garner dying in my arms. Guilt made me glance over at Esmee and I quickly averted my eyes when I realized she was staring at me inquisitively.

"You with us, Allie?" she whispered.

"Yeah, I'm good. Just trying to focus, is all. Trying to think of what Mallis might be getting out of bringing me out here."

I looked down at the crystal and it was pulsing rapidly, tugging at the silver chain that restrained it. It pointed straight ahead. We were definitely in the right place.

We rounded the last bend in the driveway and came face-to-face with the burned out ruins of the house. There was nothing left but a few charred stone pillars, a smoky brick fireplace, and a few bits of metal cabinetry that had managed to survive the inferno. Everything sat on a blackened foundation that looked entirely too small to have been the footprint for the massive home I remembered.

"Still nothing," said Cody, "maybe we lucked out."

"No such thing as luck," said Elion advancing slowly.

The charm I held flashed brightly and then died out, dropping powerless to dangle lithely in my hand.

"Okay. Looks like this has to be the spot. But I've no idea what we are looking for," I said.

There were no clouds in the sky and the moon clearly illuminated everything around us. It was great for the two of us that couldn't see in the dark, but it also meant that anything hiding out there could also see us.

"C'mon, let's get this over with and get out of here," I said, approaching the ruins up the intact brick staircase and onto the concrete foundation. "I guess just look around for anything that looks like it doesn't belong here."

"Can't you use your magic to locate the artifact?" Esmee asked.

"I can try," I said, raising my hand to draw on my power.

"I wouldn't," said Elion hastily. "If Mallis's witch has targeted you, then using your magic could activate another spell against you. We don't have your aunts here to fight it off."

As much as I hated to admit it, he was right. But the thought of being out in the open like this without my magic as backup creeped me out completely. The quicker I could find whatever it was, the quicker I could get back to the safety of the house.

We spread out, Esmee and Cody walking around the back side of the house and Elion moving slowly through the central foundation, where the staircase leading to the upper floor had once stood.

"Blood," said Elion. "I smell blood. It's coming from the fireplace."

We moved to the old brick floor-to-ceiling fireplace with a blackened stone mantle. There, sitting on the mantle, was a strange looking vial. Holding it up to the light and tilting it side to side, I could make out a murky substance swirling within.

Cody was at my side and he hissed in disgust, his

features morphing into his hybrid form. "Allie! That's your blood in there. I'd recognize that scent anywhere."

Before I could say anything else, I could see Elion stiffen and move away from us.

"Odd," said Elion, stooping to examine the foundation. He ran his fingers through the soot and raised them to his nose.

"What is it?" asked Esmee.

"This fire," he replied. "It isn't natural. It is magical in nature."

"What?" replied Esmee rushing to his side. "You mean...this wasn't an accident?"

Before anyone could answer, a voice rang out clearly from outside the house.

"Oh, come on. You mean you haven't told your friend what happened here, Allie?" We looked around just in time to see Shira materialize in the burnt lawn just outside of the house perimeter. "Oh well. I guess where she's going it won't matter what she knows." She looked at Esmee and smiled. "Say hello to the good doctor when you see her."

With that, she shifted into her wolf form and charged at us. And then about a dozen other wolves that were suddenly running beside her.

Chapter Eleven

"Goddamnit!" said Esmee. "Where the hell did they come from?"

Cloaking spell. That was the only explanation. They had been standing there the entire time and we'd walked right by them. I must have been really off my game not to have noticed that.

"They were cloaked!" I screamed. I started to summon my magic when I remembered what Elion had said before. But he had also said that I was most likely the victim of a blood magic spell, and there was blood in the vial I held in my hand. My blood. I acted on pure instinct and threw the vial into the fireplace, shattering it. Holding out one hand, I sent a blast of power into the hearth, incinerating the broken glass and remnants of my blood.

It was like a veil had been lifted from my eyes. Suddenly the space around me flared with magical markings. I looked out at the advancing hoard of werewolves and could see the black tendrils drifting off their bodies like smoke—leftover tale-tale signs of the power that had hidden their presence from us. Elion had been right. I'd been the victim of another spell, but this one was far more subtle than the last ones. It had simply dulled my mystic senses, in effect blinding me.

But now the blinders were off, and I was thoroughly pissed off. My magic flared to life as I formed two smoldering balls of blue fire around my hands. I hurled one at Shira. Snarling, she dodged it effortlessly, letting it land behind her where it exploded in a spectacular display of sound and fury. The wolves around her yelped in confusion but she quickly rallied them with a roar, and they closed in on us. With a final bound, Shira gained the foundation and was met by Cody, who had now completely shifted into his wolf form.

The sound of the two large wolves smashing into one another hit me like a physical blow. I didn't have time to react, as the wave of wolves behind her were almost on us. I threw another fireball into their midst, scattering them and knocking them off-balance. Before they could regroup, Elion and Esmee were among them.

Howls of pain rang out as Esmee's silver blade cut into flesh and sinew. For his part, Elion simply relied on pure muscle to get the job done. He grabbed the large body of the closest wolf and with a single heave, threw it into the charging pack, scattering them like so many pins before a very hairy bowling ball. The crunch of bones from the collision was sickening.

Like most supernaturals, the wolves were built to take punishment, and though hurt, they were far from incapacitated. They shrugged off their injuries and continued their advance, snarling and roaring in rage. I felt the floor shake as I turned to see Cody and Shira crash into one of the stone pillars. Shira had her jaws clamped around Cody's throat and was trying to get enough leverage to deliver a killing bite.

Without thinking, I hurled a bolt of blue lightning her way. It struck her in the flank and sent her reeling head over heals away from Cody. Cody looked at me, blood seeping from the wound on his neck. His eyes suddenly narrowed and he roared at me in warning. I spun around just in time to see one of the other wolves lunging at me. I again summoned power, this time forming it into a whip that curled around the leaping werewolf, catching him in midair. I pulled my arm back over my head, taking the wolf with it, and then snapped it down, crashing the beast into the concrete flooring. I heard his hip and spine shatter on impact. The thing was dead before it knew what had happened.

"Esmee! Throw it!" I screamed.

She didn't hesitate, raising her arm and throwing her rapier at a group of wolves with all the strength she could muster. I focused my magic on the blade, sending a bolt of charging force into the spinning silver. The effect was electrifying. The blade glowed with my magic and cut through four of the werewolves with lethal consequence. Muscle, sinew, and bone burst into pieces as the blade whirled through the air, leaving a spray of dark blood in its wake, before arching around and returning to Esmee's hand.

"Holy shit!" she said. "You have got to make that a regular feature!" She again leapt at the closest wolf and began swinging the blade at the creature, forcing it back.

Elion waded back into the pack as well. This time, he had willed his own nails to elongate into an approximation of claws and he swung them with deadly efficiency, raking through the thick hide of the wolves, throwing streaks of red everywhere.

I heard more roars coming from the woods that flanked the house, and a moment later more wolves were pouring out of the covering, sprinting towards us. They were moving fast and there were more than I could count. *Damnit*! What had we walked into?

I stretched both hands out at my side and brought them together in front of me in a thunderous clap. Blue lightning crackled forth, spidering outward and striking the advancing army, incinerating those that it hit. But they were quickly replaced with more bodies as a seemingly endless horde advanced on us. This time, they began to zigzag as they ran, making it hard for me to hit them.

I heard more snarling from behind and turned to see Shira, now in hybrid form, wrestling with Cody. She had his large wolf body in a bear hug and I heard his ribs snapping as he yelped in pain. I readied a bolt of fire to throw at her, but as soon as I raised my hand to aim at her, she dropped Cody and sprinted at me with supernatural speed. I barely had time to get a shield up in front of me before she crashed headlong into it. She backed up, curled her hand into a fist and threw a powerful blow against my shield.

I had forgotten just how monstrously strong she was. I gritted my teeth and threw more energy into reinforcing my shield. My mind raced as I thought of spells that might work against an enraged alpha werewolf. "I thought you were maimed. Where'd you get the new paw?"

She snarled and half laughed, half barked at me. "You're a fool, little girl. Don't you know that werewolves heal exceptionally fast? If we lose a limb, another, stronger one grows back in its place." She held up her hand, fingers splayed, before again curling it into a fist and landing another devastating blow on my shield. The impact rocked me backwards but my shield held. "I should thank you. Or perhaps I'll just repay you in kind."

She stepped back and glared at me before shifting into her full wolf form. Hurling her massive weight against me, her strategy was clear: use brute force to batter her way through my shields. Yeah. Good luck with that. I wasn't afraid of my shield breaking, but the longer I was engaged with her, the less help I would be to my friends. Time to go on the offense.

Shira backed up and prepared to launch herself at me again. This time I was ready for her. I willed my shield to morph into a crackling blue net that I threw over her, ensnaring her. She roared in defiance and rage as I tightened the magic around her. I poured more magic into the construct, reinforcing it against her snapping teeth. Then I lifted the net and its thrashing cargo and swung it against one of the stone pillars. The impact shattered the column but did not illicit the back-breaking response I was hoping for.

She was definitely stronger than she used to be. And was it just my imagination, or was she also bigger than I remembered? Her wolf form was larger even than Cody's at this point. I gritted my teeth and swung again, this time up and down against the concrete foundation like I had done with the other wolf. Still, I accomplished little more than knocking the breath out of her—the effort was winding me more than it was her.

Again she shifted back into her hybrid form and roared at me. Then she grabbed the netting in two places, hands in front of her, and began to pull her arms in opposite directions, trying to rip her way out. The strain on me was considerable and I could feel the sweat breaking out on my forehead. I could try another direct lightning strike. At this range, it should fry her. But that would mean dropping the shield, and as fast as Shira was, did I really want to do that? Damnit, she didn't even seem to be breathing hard!

Wait! That was it!

I brought my hands together in front of me, tracing a circle in the air. In response, my net solidified into a single glowing sphere around Shira's head. At first she seemed confused, but then I saw the light of realization hit her.

She may have been incredibly strong, but even a werewolf needed oxygen. I concentrated on the sphere, making it contract closer to Shira's head. She was using up the air inside the bubble, and the sphere prevented her from getting fresh oxygen to replace it. This time her roar was one of frantic desperation as she clawed at the construct that was slowly cutting her off from the life-sustaining air around her.

To her credit, she didn't try shifting to her wolf form. Maybe that would have required too much energy for her. Instead, she dropped to her knees and slammed her head into the solid foundation with a deafening crack. Again and again she reared back, trying to break my magic. But I had her this time, and I could feel each blow becoming weaker and weaker until she finally fell gasping onto her back, struggling in vain to pull in more oxygen.

Finally, she shifted once again. But not into her wolf form—rather, her hybrid self slid effortlessly back into human shape. She lay there, covered in sweat and barely breathing. Once again I willed the globe to contract, forcing the last reserves of air from her body. I was concentrating hard on what I was doing. Too hard. I didn't hear the attack come from behind.

I sensed it too late. Another wolf plowed into me and sent me spiraling to the ground and sliding across the floor, where I finally struck the fireplace with my back. Air whooshed from my lungs and silver fireworks exploded behind my closed eyelids. Moaning, I tried to roll over and force myself to all fours. I opened my eyes to try to find my attacker.

Through blurry vision, I made out a reddish-colored werewolf standing where I had been. Instead of attacking, he ran to where Shira lay and began to whimper over her form. Struggling to get to my feet, I tried to make my way over to her, oblivious to the cacophony of battle around me. I had to make sure she was dead. And if she wasn't, I needed to finish the job.

My magic was shaky at best—having the wind knocked out of you will do that. Still, I concentrated on drawing a blue flame up, and it danced on the palm of my hand as I stepped toward her. The red wolf that had attacked me eyed my approach and issued a warning growl. He placed his body between myself and Shira. His countenance let me know that he would die before he let me any closer to her.

Fine. So be it then; two for the price of one.

"Allie, look out!" screamed Elion. I turned to see the vampire launching himself through the air from over thirty feet away.

There were two more wolves that had stalked up behind me and were about to spring. Elion dropped down out of the sky like a living meteor and crashed into the wolves. He landed an elbow-smash on one of the creature's heads, shattering through bone and driving it into the ground. In one fluid motion he swung his other arm out and snatched the second wolf out of mid-air, grabbing it by the scruff of its neck. Despite the great size of the wolf, it was clear that

Elion had the advantage when it came to strength. The wolf thrashed and howled, trying desperately to free itself from Elion's grasp.

It didn't stand a chance. Elion calmly held the wolf up in front of him and then drove his free hand into its torso, and all the way through to the other side of the creature. The wolf made a single pathetic *yip* before its eyes rolled back and its head lolled to one side, tongue hanging out. Elion dropped the carcass unceremoniously and then gave me one of his creepy smiles. I nodded my thanks and turned back to Shira.

Except...there was no sign of the she-wolf or the one that had saved her. I scanned the perimeter of the house searching for any sign of them.

"Shit!" I said to no one in particular.

"Allie," said Cody sidling up next to me. He was in human form and was holding one arm across his waist, gripping his side.

"Cody! You okay?"

"I will be," he groaned. "I think that bitch broke every rib I have."

"Guys, I think we are in trouble here," said Esmee. She was walking backwards towards us, her blade held out defensively in front of her. "That is a hell of a lot of wolves surrounding us."

The darkness greeted me with dozens of glowing yellow eyes that were slowly stalking towards us. Glancing around, I saw that they were appearing on all sides. We were surrounded.

"Allie, can you beam us out of here...or whatever you do?" asked Esmee. One look at her told me that she was exhausted. There were scratches on her face and she was covered in blood. Bits of gore and bone clung to her ponytail and protective leather jacket she wore.

"I don't know if I have the energy left to create a portal for all of us!" I had expended a lot of magic trying to kill Shira. I could feel the reserves refilling but I still needed a moment to catch my breath before I could attempt another big spell. And judging by how close the werewolves were, I didn't think we had a moment left.

Beside me, Cody shifted to his full wolf-form and unleashed a thunderous *roar*. Esmee, breathing hard, raised her blade and squared her shoulders. Elion focused on the wolves behind us and began to growl back at them. He was going full vamp on us. Not only were his nails extended, but I could also make out the white of his fully-extended fangs, which he now bared as he eyed the advancing pack.

If the wolves were afraid, they didn't show it. As one, they howled and sprang at us, all fang and claw and bloodlust.

I raised my hands, trying to summon the energy to erect a barrier. But before I could even touch on my magic, the air around us was split by an ear-rupturing shriek.

Everything around us was suddenly whipping up at what felt like gale-force winds. The werewolves stopped in their charge, clearly as distracted as we were. Then, without warning, the sound of giant wings flapping joined the powerful shrieks of wind, buffeting our ears. A shadow crossed the sky, briefly blotting out the moon's light. I looked up in time to see a giant harpy eagle descend on the lead pack of wolves that was closest to us.

Austin dropped out of the sky like a dive-bomber, talons extended before her. She landed on one of the wolves, pinning him to the ground. The wolf snarled in surprise, but twisted and landed a bite on Austin's leg. In response, the great bird lunged forward, driving her beak into the werewolf's chest. The popping of bone could be heard by everyone around them as she snapped her beak around his still-beating heart and wrenched it free of his chest.

Instantly, more wolves were on her, leaping and attacking, trying to land a bite on her wings. Austin cried out in response and used her powerful wings as battering rams as she tried to swat the creatures back. As she swept aside their attacks, she launched into her own offense, snapping at the wolves and ripping into them with her razor-sharp talons.

The shock of the sight quickly wore off, allowing us to turn our attention to the wolves that were still charging from behind. I sent a volley of blue fire into their midst, singeing the ones I could. Elion and Cody rushed the wolves, meeting them head-on with claws and fangs. A roar erupted from behind that was so loud that I knew it wasn't Cody. Leaping into the pack, Jhamal tore into the wolves, biting and ripping with all the power his lion possessed.

Elion's form blurred as he sprinted to the great lion's side. He grabbed one of the wolves that had managed to lodge himself on Jhamal's haunches and pulled the creature away from him. He twisted to the side and drove the werewolf into the ground. Straddling the surprised shifter, he sunk his teeth into the wolf's neck, ignoring the sharp yelps it elicited. Within seconds the wolf grew still. Elion reared back and offered up his own roar to the moon, blood that looked black coating his face and running down his chest.

I fired up more of my magic, determined to take full advantage of the distraction and route these monsters.

That's when they all stopped attacking. As a unit they began to retreat, silently slinking back from the fray. I heard one lone howl, long and piercing, echoing all around us. Someone was calling for a retreat.

Shira.

At least I thought it was a retreat.

"Allie," whispered Cody next to me, "something is very wrong." He was sniffing the air ahead of us, a warning growl echoing out of his deep chest.

Elion appeared next to me, fangs still fully extended. "We need to go. Now!"

"What is it?" I asked. His eyes were fixed on something in the treeline straight ahead. I followed his gaze.

There was a slight orange glow creeping through the trees. As it got closer I could see the undergrowth and saplings beginning to burn. Slowly, an immense figure appeared and stepped into the clearing. At first I thought it was a large wolf. But then I realized it wasn't quite shaped like a wolf. The body was definitely that of a canine, close to six and a half feet tall at the shoulders. It was massively muscled and looked to be the size of a small SUV; it had to weigh at least a ton. The head was massive, more like that of a giant mastiff than the long, sleek muzzle of a wolf. It was meant to take a beating and not flinch. There was a thick tuft of fur that grew around the head that made me think of Jhamal's mane. The same tufted formation grew down the beast's legs from below the knees, flowing out to cover the feet. Even through that hair I could see the glint of incredibly sharp claws peeking out from paws that were more than twice the size of a human hand.

Of course, the other thing that set the creature apart from the other werewolves was the flames. It looked like it was on fire, with red and orange fire covering it from head to toe. Even at this distance, I could hear the crackle as they danced in the air around it. Its huge head lowered as it stalked forward. Its eyes burned the same reddish fire as the flames surrounding it, and steam hissed from its open maw.

"That," said Elion, "is a hellhound."

"Holy shit," said Esmee backing up. "What do we do?"

"You run," said Elion calmly. "Get everyone back to your house and make sure your wards are up."

"What about you?" I asked.

"That thing can easily keep pace with your vehicle. I'll distract it long enough for you to get away."

"Elion, it's almost dawn," I said, giving him a knowing glance.

"I'll be okay. But now isn't the time for you to lose half your team. And if you try to fight that beast that is exactly what will happen."

"I'm going with you," growled Cody as he prepared to shift from hybrid to full wolf.

"No you're not," said Elion. "You need to stay close to Allie. If they are risking the hound at this point in time, then Mallis's end game is near. He's going to start pressing on all fronts. Protect her and her aunts, that's who he will start to target now."

With that, he was gone, sprinting in a blur towards the hellhound.

"C'mon!" I yelled. "Everybody out of here! Austin, Jhamal, get back to the house as quickly as possible. We're outta here! Cover your eyes, people!"

I raised both hands overhead and summoned a ball of light. Then I threw it into the retreating wolves behind us where it exploded in a shower of white sparks that rained down on the shapeshifters. Temporarily stunning them, it gave us enough time to run from the back of the burnt house and towards the long winding drive that would take us back to the car.

Austin provided more coverage for us as she flew low, her powerful wings whipping the air into a frenzy and further scattering the wolves, before she arched gracefully into the sky and out of sight. Jhamal simply ran, easily outpacing any wolves that may have tried to give chase. Esmee, Cody and myself made it back to the Navigator unscathed.

"Hang on!" said Esmee as she gunned the big vehicle, turning it towards home.

Chapter Twelve

"We shouldn't have left him!" said Cody.

The house was surprisingly quiet as we entered. I slammed the door behind us and mentally checked to make sure the wards around the house were operating at peak efficiency. As I suspected, Jhamal and Austin had beaten us home.

"And what were you two doing there?" Cody continued. He was clearly agitated.

"Ummm, saving your asses, in case you hadn't noticed," replied Austin.

"Allie was clear when she told you to stay behind! So much for having the element of surprise when the time comes to reveal the Totem Shifters."

"It was my fault," said Jhamal. "I was planning to sneak out and follow you. In my lion form I can track you guys almost anywhere. Austin caught me sneaking out and wanted to come along as well."

"I was backup to his backup," she said. "Just in case shit got too real."

"And not for nothing, but it looked like we showed up at just the right time," said Jhamal.

"What is going on down here?" said Aunt Vivian from the stairway, making her way down.

Gar and Hope entered the room as well, rubbing their eyes sleepily.

"What's going on is that Jhamal and Austin crashed our little party tonight after they were told to stay here," said Cody.

"It's okay, Cody," I said. "And they're right. We should be thanking them. If they hadn't shown up when they did... we might not be here right now."

Gar gave Jhamal a horrified look before turning and stalking out of the room. Jhamal took a deep breath and ran after him.

"Jesus, are you okay?" said Hope to Esmee. "Is that... blood all over you?"

"Yeah," Esmee replied. "But don't worry, it's not mine. Well, at least most of it isn't."

"Wait, where is Elion?" Hope asked.

"He stayed behind to create a diversion so the rest of us could get out. We were attacked by Shira and a whole lot of werewolves," I said. "And a hellhound. Elion took on the hound so we could get away."

"My God," said Hope, "is he...?"

"I don't know," I said. "He saved my life once during the fight. And then he risked himself to save the rest of us."

"And as a thanks, we left him behind," said Cody.

"Cody, what is going on with you? He made the call that I'm sure you also would have if you'd been in his shoes. I know I sure as hell would have done the same thing."

He didn't reply but instead began to pace the living room.

"You know what?" said Hope taking Esmee by the arm, "let's get you out of these and into a hot shower. You smell." She eyeballed me as she guided Esmee away and I breathed a silent "thank you" to her.

"Okay, talk," I said. "You don't even like Elion. Why are you so worried about him right now?"

"Because I want...no, I *need* to finish talking to him about what he was saying on the way over. I need to know that he is lying about why I was created."

I looked from Cody to Aunt Vivian. "We had been led to believe that the werewolves were created by the vampires to help protect them during the day. But Elion said they were created to hunt witches."

"He said that was why I was drawn to you Allie," said Cody. "If that's true..."

"No," I said. "No matter why werewolves were originally created, that isn't the reason you and I are together now."

"He didn't say it, Allie, but he implied that at some point I might actually hurt you."

"That won't happen," I said. I walked over to him and placed a hand on his cheek. "I have the utmost trust in you. That will never change."

"What about your first attack...when you said you were pulled out of your body? You said my wolf was there..."

"Tricks and subterfuge," said Aunt Vivian. "The witch was probably messing with Allie's head. Trying to sow seeds of doubt and fear."

"And it didn't work," I said, looking at Aunt Vivian. I was glad that she had said this, but I knew my aunts well enough to know when they were lying.

"Allie, what did you find?" Aunt Vivian said, trying to get us back on track.

"Blood. My blood in a vial at the site of the old Fischer place."

Aunt Vivian nodded and then sat down on the couch. "So it was blood magic that the witch was working. She was able to create spells that were geared to you alone; that explains how she was able to pull your astral self out of your body like that. Nasty stuff. Did you destroy it?"

"Yes. Hopefully there wasn't any more," I said.

"It was a trap. Shira attacked and meant to kill us all," said Cody. "And that hound…Jesus."

"The good news is that the spell that created the totem shifters seems to have worked better than I could have expected," I said. "You should have seen Austin tear into the werewolves. It was very impressive."

Cody nodded. "They will definitely be a strong addition to the team. Still, I'm sure by now Mallis has received word that there is something more at play now than just run-of-the-mill shifters."

"Doesn't matter," I said. "Elion was right. Judging from the size of the forces that attacked us, he's determined to take us out before the eclipse. Gloves are off: we need to be prepared for anything at this point."

"Something still doesn't feel right," said Cody. "I mean, if he was willing to throw that many werewolves at us, then he has to have way more in reserves. Why wouldn't he have attacked us before? The eclipse is right around the corner. Why wait till the last minute to try and get rid of us?"

"Maybe he realizes that brute force won't get the job done," offered Aunt Vivian. "He needs to take out Allie. That's where the blood magic attack came in. It takes time to create a spell like that. He obviously has a very skilled witch working for him, but he can't risk her in a direct confrontation with us until she completes the Leveling spell."

"Possible," I said. "But he also has the Warlock as well. I would think he would at least have put in an appearance at some point. He seems to have been a pivotal part of Mallis's plans up until now."

"'Up until now' may be the key part of that statement," said Aunt Vivian. "Perhaps, now that Mallis has a true witch at his side, he no longer needs a pale imitation."

Harsh as it may have sounded, it was true. If magic was what the vampire needed to bring about his plans, then having a witch on his side made his job one thousand times easier. It also reduced his exposure to danger, as he no longer needed to risk capturing witches for the Warlock to use as a battery.

"Another thing: why would they have picked that particular site to set up a trap? No way was it just a random coincidence that the witch was using that burned out house as a hiding place for an artifact to bounce her magic off," I said.

"No," agreed Cody, "that was planned and staged. But why?"

"I'd like to know that as well," said Esmee. She walked back into the room dressed in a thick, blue bathrobe. She scrubbed at her hair with a towel like her life depended on it.

"That was a quick shower," I said a little too hastily. "Do you need to go lie down?"

"Thank you, but I'd rather hear the end of this conversation." She plopped down on the couch next to Aunt Vivian and focused on Cody and I. "Elion said that the fire hadn't been natural, that it smelled like magic. Was it from that hellhound? Was that thing what killed Isla's aunt?"

No more secrets, I reminded myself. "No. It wasn't."

"Allie…" Cody said.

"No, it's okay. This is something I should have told sooner." I took a deep breath and walked over to sit on the large ottoman that doubled as a coffee table. I wanted to be at eye level with Esmee. "The fire that destroyed Dr. Garner's home was magical in nature. I did it. I…we…were there that night."

Esmee's body went rigid as her eyes hardened. "Did you…Allie, did you kill her?"

"What? No! God, no, Esmee. That was Shira. Cody and I were following up on a lead that led us to Dr. Garner. She was attacked by the Order and Shira while we were there. She died fighting them."

"Why were they there to begin with?" asked Esmee.

God, I was hoping that she would not ask that. "I'm not exactly sure. But—and I can't prove this—she knew what was going on with the Order rounding up all of the scattered wolf siblings. She was working with them to get the parents to bring the wolves in…"

My words dangled in the air and I could see Esmee trying to digest what I had said.

"Esmee, whatever her reason for being there, I really believe she was doing the right thing. She had been helping to take care of the wolves since they were first adopted by humans. She was trying to help keep them safe in the long run. She died helping us live."

"And as a thanks, you burned her body?" Esmee said, her voice quivering.

My voice caught in my throat. "I…in all honesty, I didn't know what to do. She had been attacked by a supernatural. I didn't know if she would turn into…something, or maybe rise again as a weapon of the Order. I wasn't going to take a chance on any of that happening."

She didn't speak but I could see the questions forming in her mind. I didn't need telepathy to tell what she was thinking.

"I haven't told Isla, if that's what you're wondering," I said.

"Of course not. We don't have secrets."

I nodded because I knew what that meant—I could only hope that Isla would understand, and if she didn't, that she'd ask me why. She and Esmee had become more than just my partners in this fight; they were my friends. Keeping this from Isla had been eating me alive, and I felt like a weight had been lifted off my shoulders.

"So what now?" Cody asked breaking the tension. "As far as our next steps, I mean."

"We rest for a couple of hours, and then we head out and see if we can't pick up Elion's trail. I don't want to go out now because we can't risk the wolves still being up and about. Let's go a couple hours after sunrise."

"I'm going home," said Esmee. I looked at her, not bothering to hide my hurt. She came over and gave me a hug. "I'm not leaving because of what was just said. But because I don't like the thought of Isla being left alone. They know where we live."

"I'm going with you," said Jhamal, walking back into the room.

"Jhamal," I said, "how's Gar?"

"He understands why I went. Doesn't make him any happier about it, but he gets it. Still, I think a day apart will do us some good." He smiled and walked over to Esmee and placed a hand on her shoulder. "Ready when you are."

Aunt Vivian gave both of them a hug, as did Cody and I, before they headed out the door.

"Whatever you do," said Esmee before heading for her car, "be careful. Call me if you need anything."

I promised I would and waved as they eased out of the driveway. I was just about to lock the door when I noticed another car pulled up to the house. It was a four-wheel drive Wrangler that I didn't recognize.

Cody joined me at the door, and together we watched as two people got out of the car and made their way up the walkway.

"Who's that?" Cody asked.

"Nate. He's one of the new totem shifters. He went to get a friend earlier, someone he feels that may be a help to us."

"I thought Otherkind were...I don't know...not daddy level hot," Cody said into my ear.

I smiled and greeted Nate warmly, introducing him to both Cody and Aunt Vivian, who was just on her way back to bed.

"This is my friend, Rob," he said, indicating the man who entered the house behind him. His friend was probably in his mid-forties. His hair was black peppered with gray. It was cut short but still a little unkempt. His face was lined with the evidence of his age and had the hardened, bronzed look of someone that has stayed out in the sun longer than they probably should have. His eyes were bright blue and sparkled with intensity as he took my hand, shaking it vigorously in a firm grip.

"So you're the witch," Rob said. I knew instantly that subtlety wasn't going to be his strong point, and I immediately liked him as a result.

"Um, yeah that would be me. And this is my boyfriend, Cody."

He shook Cody's hand with the same vigor and stared

him in the eye. "Heard about you, too. You're the werewolf, right? Cool. We might have some things in common."

"Oh?" said Cody. "What is your Kintype, if I may ask?"

"I'm a grey muzzle," Rob replied. "A wolf."

"Yeah, I always take him for a big old teddy bear, personally," laughed Nate as he playfully ruffled Rob's hair, then danced away before the faux punches Rob tossed at his midsection could land. "But yeah, he's a grizzled old wolf. One of my first friends I ever made when I came out as Otherkin. He was one of the first in our community."

I marveled at the respect the two obviously had for one another.

"So, you can make me whole?" Rob said expectantly.

"I hope so. You know what I am asking in return, right?"

"I do. And trust me, I have no problem paying in full if I can experience what Nate has. Even if it's just once."

"The spell will be permanent. You'll be able too shift whenever you want to" I said. "I just hope you're ready. And, I hate to throw you into the fire, but time is of the essence here. I need your help, Nate." I felt Cody bristle, but ignored it.

"What can I...we, do for you?"

"We need to leave soon. We're going to track a hellhound."

Chapter Thirteen

Breakfast was quickly whipped up. Giant platters of bacon, eggs and biscuits with an assortment of jams and marmalades were placed out buffet style. Gar really had thought this through. He had stockpiled not only the main fridge, but the second one in the basement as well. Our guests certainly weren't going to go hungry anytime soon.

He had rallied the troops sleeping in the mystically expanded attic, set up the table, and cooked breakfast, all so our aunts could sleep in. Plus, I'm pretty sure he wanted to show them that he could to the heavy lifting when it came to hosting a bunch of Otherkin that he had invited for a sleepover. Personally, I was happy he was so invested in making sure everything was to everyones' liking. It made it that much easier when I told him that he couldn't follow Cody and I. He had protested, of course, but I told him that I needed him to take the Otherkind to the shifter encampment to not only introduce them, but to let them practice their new powers as well. Kendra would be able to run them through their paces and help to make sure that they were ready when the time came.

Cody agreed with the plan, knowing how important it was for me to keep my family safe, but also realizing that if we were going to have a shot at winning this, we would need the totems to be as comfortable with their powers as possible. Ideally, I would have sent Nate and Rob along with them...but at the same time if we ran into that hellhound, a saber-toothed tiger might come in handy.

It had taxed me further than I would have liked to admit to turn Rob. His Kintype was stubborn and didn't want to come out at first. But I coaxed gently, didn't run roughshod over him. It reminded me of the time our aunts had brought a puppy home for Gar and I after we first lost our mother. The poor thing had been transported in a small pet carrier and had cried continuously. Gar and I wanted to reach into the crate and pull it out immediately, but Aunt Lena cautioned us against doing that.

"No, no...let him come to you," she said. "He was just dragged away from his mother and put into a crate and shipped halfway across the country. He is alone and scared, and right now the only safe space he knows is that carrier."

She then set the carrier in the garage, opened the door, and asked us to sit in front of the crate. We did as she told us, offering soothing words of encouragement to the little fella, letting him know with reassuring whispers that we weren't a threat. I'll never forget when his little black and white head finally emerged, and he took those first tentative steps into the light and into our lives. Thinking about him made my eyes tear up. He was a great, beloved member of our family and it was rough when old age finally claimed him. Gar had cried for weeks when he passed, and so had I.

And just like we were rewarded with a lifetime of

loyalty from our gigantic husky/shepherd mix, so too I was hoping for equal loyalty from Rob's wolf. Like the man himself, the wolf appeared old and grizzled, but very powerful. A gray and black coat covered a body larger even than Cody's wolf. Unlike the other totem shifters that often took on unnatural hues, Rob retained his same blue eyes. They were surprisingly human, and there was no mistaking the cunning and intelligence behind them.

Rob was our only canine shifter, and my hope was that between he and Nate, we would be able to get a fix on where Elion had gone and what may have happened to him. And if we managed to find him? Hopefully, that was where Nate and Cody would come into play. The power of wolf shifters was impressive and hopefully intimidating to vampires.

There was absolutely nothing to be found on hellhounds in any of the tomes my aunts had in their considerable library. A quick search of the internet turned up nothing of use either. There were a lot of vague references to them on a supernatural television show that Gar and I liked to watch together, but nothing concrete.

Nothing that told me how to kill one.

Admittedly, I did feel a little bad for not having gone after Elion right away. He had saved my life, after all. But I needed rest and food. I wouldn't be of much use to anyone if I keeled over from exhaustion.

We headed out as soon as Gar was able to get everyone into their vehicles, and headed over to the shifter encampment. I gave Kendra a heads up as to what was going on. Of course she wanted to come with us, but I told her I needed her to work with the totem shifters and get a feel for their strengths and weaknesses.

We drove in silence back towards Dr. Garner's house in Nate's surprisingly comfortable jeep.

"So, a hellhound huh?" said Rob. "Is that a different kind of shifter as well?"

"I'm not sure," I replied. "There are no records of what exactly it is. I don't get the feeling it's a shifter, however. More like…a creature in and of itself. Something from the dark dimension that Mallis was somehow able to pull through."

"Whatever it is, it is very, very big," said Cody. "And did you see the way the fire around it burned?" He turned to me with concern in his eyes.

"Yes. It scorched the ground where it walked, but seemingly in a controlled pattern."

"So when—or if—we find this thing, what do we do?" asked Nate.

"We fight," said Cody.

"Okay, well first let's just concentrate on finding Elion," I said. "Then we'll worry about hellhounds. It's daylight, so that means Elion would have gone to ground."

"You're assuming he's still alive," said Cody. "Or that the hound didn't drag him off and present him as a gift to Mallis."

That was something I hadn't thought about. I certainly didn't want to think of Elion as being dead, but it had never even occurred that he might be a prisoner somewhere. I prayed that wasn't the case. Cody and I had been there and done that; it wasn't something I wished on anyone.

We arrived at the house and made our way up to the ruins. It looked like what it was: the remnants of a battle scene. The stone pillars that had been standing were mostly smashed to rubble, and the area around the house was now as charred as the foundation. My fire had reduced much of the tall grass to patches of smoldering blackness. Streaks of red blotted large swaths of the landscape. But despite the considerable gore, there was one thing missing.

"Where are the bodies?" asked Cody, echoing my thoughts.

We had killed a lot of wolves last night, yet there was no sign of them anywhere. I walked to a corner of the ruins and surveyed a huge section that was covered in dried blood. This was where Esmee had gone all Cuisinart on a few of them, and blood was streaking the brick fireplace.

But again, no bodies or even parts of bodies. I did a quick magical scan of the area to make sure what we were seeing was real. Yep, no sign of dead wolves anywhere.

"Would they have retrieved their dead?" asked Rob. "I mean, you said they were an army. Isn't that what armies do? I wouldn't leave the fallen body of a comrade."

"I guess that's possible," I said. "I have to stop thinking of them as animals."

Cody shot me a quick look. "Animals?"

My cheeks burned as I turned to him. "No, that's not what I meant. I meant in the heat of the moment last night...they were so..."

"So were we, Allie. You do what you have to." He turned and headed off towards the opening in the tree line where the hellhound had first appeared. I ignored Nate's furrowed brow and motioned for them to follow.

"What's your magic tell you about these burns?" said Cody. He was crouched where the hound had been standing.

The ground around us was mostly intact with green grass, and even some of the drier weeds that crackled underfoot were undisturbed. The only oddity was a repeating pattern of equally spaced areas of discoloration roughly a foot in diameter every four to five feet. They led back into the woods. Every few yards there was a patch of undergrowth that was singed away in a manner that created a set of rounded patterns on the ground.

"This was where it walked," said Cody. "It came out of the woods and then stood here." He pointed to the earth that was seared down to the red clay dirt.

I stooped down and placed my hand on one of the burned areas, closed my eyes, and concentrated. Instantly, I could feel the pain the earth had experienced when the hound had stepped on it. The ground itself was cold to the touch, the opposite of what I was expecting. But it was more than just cold. It felt barren—like it had been salted. I knew that nothing would ever again grow where this monster had walked.

Pushing aside the feelings of revulsion at what had been done to the earth, I tried to dive deeper. Past the pain and into the creature. My magic flowed, grasping, clawing at any leftover mystical signatures that may have been left behind. I could feel the cold that this beast generated. Soul-numbing, unlike anything I had ever felt before. But other than the general anemic feel I was getting from the surroundings, there was nothing else concrete for my magic to latch onto.

"Nothing," I said. "I can feel how every living thing around it recoils from this beast's touch, but I can't get a bead on the hound itself. It's like…it's shielded from my magic for some reason."

"Over here," said Rob. He had moved about fifty feet to the left. The forest was in completely different shape there. The undergrowth was flattened, and the earth had been gouged out in places with rough clumps of rock and debris scattered everywhere. "This is where they fought."

I could see it now. "Elion leapt at the beast and was met in mid-air by the hound. They landed here and battled," continued Rob. He moved slowly further to his left, concentrating on the ground around him. There were trees here that were bent and snapped, along with still more burned-out areas. "Whoever your friend is, he gave as good as he got." He pointed at a place that was saturated with red.

"Is that Elion's blood, or that of the hounds?" wondered Nate.

"That's vampire blood," said Cody, wrinkling his nose. "There is no mistaking that scent. Both of you might want to memorize it."

Unlike Cody, the totem shifters could not access their Kintype abilities or senses while in human form. They both shifted fully to their totems and began to sniff at the ground. I could hear Cody's sharply-drawn breath at the sight of them; this was his first glimpse of Nate's totem and I could tell he was impressed with the sheer size of the saber-tooth.

Rob was equally as impressive. Though not as big as Nate, he was formidable nonetheless. The two of them prowled the area, learning to isolate the smell they were tracking from those that permeated the forest. I noticed their bodies stiffen as they looked off simultaneously in the same direction.

"Yes!" said Cody. "That's it!"

Together, the two totems bounded off into the deeper woods behind the remains of the house. Nate came to a sudden halt, then bounded back to where I stood with Cody. He turned his head to the side and stared at me, a low, warm rumble emanating from his chest. I understood instantly what he wanted and vaulted onto his back, wrapping my hands in a handful of velvety hair to keep my balance.

The landscape began to blur as we headed across the open field, racing at a dizzying speed to catch up to Rob. I looked over my shoulder at Cody, who, despite his smaller wolf form, was keeping pace with the much larger totem shifters.

His eyes were narrowed and focused, but they avoided my own. I turned my attention back to the forest floor that the large, powerful cat beneath me was devouring—but then he stopped suddenly, and I had to tighten my grip to keep from flying off. Rob and Cody circled in front of us and sniffed the ground. Instantly, Cody shifted back to human form and looked up at me.

"The trail stops here. It's like the vampire just… disappeared."

I dismounted and Nate and Rob shifted back to human form as well.

"Can he do that?" asked Rob. "Disappear, I mean. In the movies some of them can fly. Maybe he just flew away."

"No. I don't think he can fly," I said. Focusing my magic, I closed my eyes and hummed a spell of clarity. When I opened them, the area shifted into a spectrum that only I could perceive. I could see Elion's presence. My magic allowed me to see that his pain was palpable as a red mist crept across the forest floor. I followed it until we came to a small glen with a dried-up creek bed.

I had no idea how long it had been since water had flown here, but the red mist now crept over the exposed river rock and made its way towards an embankment of tangled roots curving from the trees above into the ground below. They created a natural barrier that concealed dark openings that burrowed into the high banks along the dead creek.

Either Elion was in there, or something hellish had killed him and dragged his body into one of the sheltered openings.

"Something smells dead," said Cody, wrinkling his nose and turning away from the opening.

I called up a magical shield and used it to push the roots aside and widen the hole. The earth around the opening appeared to have been clawed open, creating a small cavern in the sand and rock hillside. The smell of rotten flesh hit us again. Whatever was in there was not going to be pleasant.

I lit a ball of blue light in my hand and looked back at Cody. The opening was not big enough for an adult to enter. At least, not an adult male...so guess what? It was my lucky day. I took a deep breath and pushed through the murk in the damp space.

Chapter Fourteen

I made sure to breathe through my mouth as I crawled into the tunnel. Still, the smell clawed its way into my throat and threatened to make me retch.

"Allie, what do you see?" Cody called out from behind me.

"Nothing. It's nearly pitch black in here even with my magic." I had only managed to crawl about six feet into the hole, but I might as well have been in one of the underground caverns at Singing Falls. No ambient light crept into the space, and the wet, mildewy earth surrounding me made me feel claustrophobic. For some reason, the closeness, the smell, and the soft, mushy wetness all around me made me think that this was what it would feel like to be swallowed alive.

I shuddered and put that mental image out of my mind. My hand landed in something slick and pulpy that felt like it was covered in...fur.

"Oh, fuck this," I muttered to myself, and conjured a

small ball of light that I commanded to float in front of me, illuminating the ground and immediate space.

I regretted the light almost immediately. I could finally see what I had put my hand into, and stifled a small scream. It was an opossum...or what was left of one. It looked like it had been turned inside out, guts and entrails where its skin should have been, a row of sharp, jagged teeth splintered and busted outward in all directions. It looked like the poor thing had bit down with all its strength on a metal pipe, and as a result had shattered its teeth. And exploded from the inside.

My hand was covered in the creature's remnants, and cursing my luck I wiped it on my jeans. Willing my light closer to the ground, I examined my surroundings closer before I tried to crawl further. The opossum wasn't alone. Suddenly I could see that the flooring around me was littered with carcasses of small woodland creatures. Moles, rats, squirrels...and something bigger that looked like a newborn fawn. All of them were in the same state: savaged and ripped apart. Before I could think about pushing further into the tight space, I heard a rustling to my right.

Throwing myself against the far side of the space to my left, I cast my light in the direction of the sound.

Someone—or something—was pressed against the far wall opposite me. It was camouflaged perfectly against the black earth. Roots that grew through the ground stretched downward in front of it, looking like nature's prison bars.

"Leave. Now!" came a hoarse voice. "I don't know if I can control myself."

Realization struck me like a physical blow. "Elion? Oh my God, is that you?"

The vampire only hissed in return. He turned his head away from my light but I could still make out his huddled, emaciated form. Every inch of his skin was black, and when he hissed at me again I could see that even his teeth were charred. He looked for all the world like a living skeleton that had been dipped in tar and left to harden.

"Jesus, what happened to you?" I reached out a hand tentatively in his direction.

He snarled suddenly, snapping his black teeth at my hand. I drew back, shrieking involuntarily.

"Allie!" It was Cody, screaming at me from the entrance. "What happened? I'm coming in!" I could hear him shift into his wolf form and begin to gouge hunks of earth away from the opening, trying to enlarge it enough that his massive body would fit through.

"Cody, no!" I screamed, sending a wave of magic his way that shielded the entrance, keeping him from being able to enter. "Stay where you are! Please. I'm okay."

I then turned my attention back to Elion and held up my hand in front of him. The blue glow of magic that emanated from me let him know that while I was not here to hurt him, I wouldn't be afraid to torch his ass either if I had to.

"Elion, it's me, Allie. I'm here to help you."

"I know who you are. And like I said, you should go." He turned his face away from me, pressing it into the wet wall around him, trying desperately to meld into the dirt around us.

"Elion, what happened? Cody is with me. We came to find you…" I wanted to be as reassuring as possible that we were there to help.

He growled low in his throat, but it sounded more like a cry of pain than a threat.

"Allie, please. I…I don't think I can control my

hunger…you're in danger right now just by being so close to me. I can smell the blood flowing inside you…"

"Elion…did you do this?" I asked gesturing at the carcasses all around us.

"I did. It's an old vampire trick. We can call out mentally to creatures of simple intellect and draw them to us. But…"

"But what?"

"It wasn't enough. I can't heal from them."

"What happened to you? Let me help you."

"If you want to help me, then leave me."

Slowly, I stretched my hand outward again. I tempered my magic, concentrating on creating a soothing, warm glow that I stretched over Elion's damaged body. I probed lightly at him, trying to see if there was a way to potentially heal him. My magic recoiled almost as soon as it touched him. Whatever had been done to him was so anathema to me that I had to suppress my own instincts to blast him out of his misery.

"See?" he said. "Your magic knows what you are too stubborn to admit. I'm a danger right now."

His charred skin was still smoking in places, yet surprisingly, he gave off no stench.

"Did the sun do this to you?" I asked. "Were you caught outside at dawn?"

He shook his head. "It wasn't the sun. It was the hellhound."

I shuddered at the sound of his voice. It was low and raspy, but I could hear the hate filling his tone.

"When I attacked the beast so that you could escape, I did everything in my power to avoid its burn. I moved as fast as I could, taking damage only on my fists where I repeatedly struck the creature. No matter where I hit it, I burned. But its flames were unlike anything I had ever experienced. While it seemed to generate the heat of the sun itself, it also felt cold. Fire that burned with the coldness of a glacier."

"And it did this to your skin?"

"No. Not directly. I fought the creature and lured it away from your friends, to the creek bed just out there." He nodded his chin in the direction of the opening. "I could sense the sun about to rise, and despite having rained down blow after blow on the hound, it was not weakening. So I gambled…trying the one weapon I had left." He opened his mouth and bared his charred teeth at me. "Leapt atop the beast and buried my fangs as deeply as possible into its neck, seeking to drain it." His voice trailed off and I waited for him to find the breath to continue. "That…was a mistake."

"What happened?"

"Everything about the beast burned, Allie. The cold fire coursed through its blood like a river of lava. When I drank deeply from it, I felt like I exploded from the inside out. Everything inside of me burned instantly. I felt my very intestines turn to ash. But to my credit, whatever I did somehow managed to hurt the monster as well. It reared up and threw me off, howling in pain. I expected it to run over and finish me off. I was certainly in no shape to fight back. But it didn't. Instead, it turned and ran off into the woods.

"And somehow I was still alive. If you could call it that. My body was cooking from the inside out…I could feel it. I managed to drag myself towards this opening and claw my way inside. I knew I was dead, and used my last remaining strength to send out a call for sustenance. I don't even remember eating these animals…I just remembered becoming aware of the smell of blood...real blood, and hearing your voice."

"God, Elion...we've come to help you; to get you out of here."

"I couldn't leave if I wanted to, Allie. I'm too weak. The slightest bit of sunlight will probably finish me off at this point. And I am too weak to survive until nightfall." He sighed, motioning me away. "I'd rather die alone, thank you. Please go."

"Yeah, that's not going to happen," I replied. "There has to be something. What if we bring you something bigger? There has to be larger game in these woods!"

He shook his head dismissively. "No, Allie, that won't work. I can feel the hound's fire still flowing inside me. I can't extinguish it...it's only a matter of time before it finishes me. Already...I can feel my consciousness fading... I'm losing my hold on my restraint...that's why I am begging you to leave me. Before I do something we will both regret."

I started to say something, but the words caught in my throat as a plan flashed through my mind. Not one of my smarter plans, but in this case I had nothing left to lose. Well, almost nothing.

"Elion, didn't you tell me that human blood is what vampires crave the most? That your bodies are geared to run on our blood and not that of animals?" He gave me a dark look, his smoking eyes narrowing at me as he nodded. "And you said it yourself, you can barely contain yourself right now, smelling my blood. Well, would that help you heal from this?"

He recoiled from me in horror, again baring his fangs as he backpedaled further against the wall, trying to pull the roots closer around him as if that would shield him against what I was suggesting.

"Would it heal you?" I asked again.

"I...I don't know," he rasped. "But it doesn't matter because I can't...I *won't*, do that."

I inched forward, ignoring my own fears. "Elion, if it means you staying alive, you have to. You said it yourself—you were able to hurt that hound. I need your strength to win this fight. And you need my blood to stay alive. The eclipse is two days away. If you really want to help us stop this and destroy Mallis, you have to do whatever is required to stay alive." I let my words sink in and I could see him contemplating what I was saying. "Plus, there is magic in my blood. That may help you recover even more of your strength. Besides," I said, pushing my sleeve up and holding my arm out to him, "I'm not asking you to do this. I'm telling you."

His black eyes fixed on mine and he slowly slid forward, reaching out a clod smoky hand to grip my arm. For a second I felt my magic flare up in response but I willed it back down.

"This will hurt," he said, leaning forward.

I expected it to feel like a bee sting, or like the sudden pinch at the doctor's office when they drew my blood. But no. It was nothing like that. Elion bit deep. It felt like I was stabbed in my arm, the sharp pain traveling through my entire body. I could actually feel his fangs grow longer as soon as they punctured my flesh. They stretched downward, breaching through my muscle and scraping bone. I grew dizzy almost immediately as blood from my body coursed to the area. He wasn't just drinking from my extremity, he was leeching blood from my entire body, somehow drawing it out like a vacuum.

I cried out and tried to draw back, but it was no use. His grip was like a vise and I knew there was no way I could break it. Furthermore, the sudden draining made me far weaker than I expected. Too weak to call up any magic to try and defend myself. I felt the darkness around me gather closer as I slumped forward, on the verge of total collapse.

But then, just as quickly as he started, Elion stopped drinking from me. Rearing his head back, he roared, before staring down at my bloody arm. I could see the struggle in his eyes as he resisted going back in for seconds. Instead, he dropped my arm and helped to steady me, rocking me back up into a sitting position. I looked down at my arm, half expecting to see a gaping wound open to the bone. But to my surprise there were only two punctures that were already beginning to heal.

"Your blood," said Elion, "is incredible!" His voice already sounded stronger, and the dimming flicker of my mystic light may have been playing tricks on my eyes but I could have sworn that his skin was starting to return to its pale, sickly pallor in places. At least now I could see the whites in his eyes when he stared at me. "I can feel it…the magic that runs in your veins…it is making me heal faster!"

"Good," I managed, rubbing at the spot on my arm he had bitten. "I think we need to get out of here. Stands to reason that if that hound survived, it may yet return. Or bring some wolves to try and finish you off."

"It's still midday, Allie…"

"Yes. But maybe, with the combination of my magic in your system, and a certain UV blocking spell I've been working on…we might be able to get you home before you get all toasty."

The look in his eyes didn't exactly speak volumes of trust in that plan, but it was all I had.

"Are you strong enough to attempt such a spell?" he said. "I fear I have taken so much from you…"

"Only one way to find out. Plus, I have a new shifter waiting outside. He's fast. Very fast. He can stick to the woods and bring you home. That will reduce your exposure even more. So unless you have a better idea…"

He looked down at his hands. They were healing, the charred areas fading into gray spots scattered across his flesh.

"We can try it. I've been burnt once already…what's one more time?"

I smiled, even though we both knew that another burn would most likely be his last. Holding out my hands, I held both of his in mine and concentrated. I created a shield around him, one that hugged his skin. Instead of my normal blue light, I created one that was almost blindingly white; it would, in theory, refract all light away from him. Hopefully, it would last long enough to get him to the safety of the house.

As I began crawling from the hole, I heard him clear his throat. "So…um, what exactly is this new speedy shifter you have?"

"Oh. It's a saber-toothed tiger."

Chapter Fifteen

Even with Nate's speed, it had been close.

His initial reaction to Elion was the same as Cody's: revulsion. Something in their supernatural DNA made their inner spidey-sense tingle uncontrollably around a vampire. I could understand. It came from untold centuries of self-preservation that were ingrained in them. Most shifters were considered apex predators in the supernatural world, but vampires were really still a step up the food chain.

Luckily, Nate's trust in me overrode his fear of Elion. He ran hard, eating up the ground between the forest and home with Elion clinging to him for dear life.

"Stay in the shadows as much as possible," I said. And to his credit, Nate did just that, clinging to the slightest of paths that hugged the tree line. Where there was no path he made one, his powerful body crashing through undergrowth and snapping small trees.

I followed, riding Rob. His wolf was larger than Cody's and could more easily accommodate my frame. Even still, I could feel him struggling to keep up with the tiger. I needed to stay in as close a proximity to Nate as possible to keep the shield around Elion at full strength. What I hadn't counted on was just how weak I would be after losing so much blood to Elion.

I was cursing myself for not thinking of that. What happened to a witch's construct if she passed out? As I faded, was my shield that protected Elion from frying fading as well? I fought the waves of dizziness that Rob's constant bounding over the landscape was causing. Instead I focused on Cody's form as he ran along beside us. He was smaller, but seemed to have no problem keeping up with the larger totem shifters.

We crashed through the final set of trees that broke out into the backyard of my house. As soon as Nate entered the yard, I used the last of my strength to throw up an umbrella cover of blue magic to reinforce the shield around Elion. With a single great leap, Nate landed on the covered lowered deck and dropped Elion before shifting back to human form. Cody and I were right behind him and together we dragged Elion inside, just as the shield I had created around him began to crackle and diffuse.

We both collapsed onto the basement floor just as my aunts hurried into the room.

"What in the world...?" began Aunt Lena. "Allie, are you okay?"

"I...I'm just a little worn out, is all."

Aunt Vivian followed her in and stopped short in her tracks when she saw me. Her eyes narrowed, and then she shifted her vision to Elion and focused her hardened gaze on him as well. "What did you do?" Her tone was scalpel-sharp.

I wasn't sure what she saw, but I knew better than to try and fib my way out of this one.

"I saved his life is what I did." I moved to one of the chairs and plopped down. For his part, Elion moved further into the basement away from the doors and to either side of the room. He edged his way towards the cool darkness of the storage room that he had made his temporary home.

"Do not play with me, girl!" Aunt Vivian said, storming up to me. "Your aura is...tainted. What did you do?"

I took what felt like the biggest breath I had ever drawn as I looked up to face my aunt. Elion spoke before I could. "The hellhound had burned me. From the inside. I was dying...it wasn't Allie's..."

"It was my choice, Aunt Vivian," I interjected. "He really was dying...I could feel it."

"No, Allie, he's already dead," said Aunt Lena. "He died centuries ago. His body just hasn't caught up to his soul yet."

"What are they talking about, Allie?" Cody asked, eyeing Elion with suspicion.

"He needed to heal," I said, "and the animals...well they weren't doing it. So I offered him some of my blood."

"You *what*?" exclaimed Cody, clenching his hands into fists as he turned to face Elion.

"Cody, stop!" I said, standing to place myself between the two men. "Like I said, I offered. And honestly, he refused it. Said he would rather have died. I practically forced it on him."

Elion stood stoically taking in the scene, his eyes soft but not leaving Cody. "She saved me. Yes, it was at great risk to herself, but without her blood I would not be here now."

Cody was fuming. HIs breath came in ragged, short bellows and I saw his eyes take on a yellow glow as he reached for his shift.

"Cody, stop it," I said, pleading with my boyfriend. "We

need him. He was able to hurt the hellhound! We will need his strength if we face that thing again."

"How?" said Aunt Lena.

"Umm, how what?" I asked, genuinely confused.

"How did you hurt the hellhound?" She had turned to face Elion now.

"I bit it," said Elion matter-of-factly. "It was proving to be impervious to brute force. No matter how hard I hit the beast, it didn't seem to slow it down. Finally, in desperation I admit, I turned to my one tried and true weapon." He bared a single fang here for emphasis.

"Did you only bite, or did you drink from the beast?" asked Aunt Lena.

Elion furrowed his brow. "I drank from him. It was instinctive to try and weaken him. That was a mistake because his blood was like liquid fire and it instantly began to sear my insides."

"What is it, sister?" said Aunt Vivian. "What are you thinking?"

"I'm thinking…we borrow a page out of Mallis's own book. He had his witch attack Allie using her blood. What's to say we can't try a similar tactic?"

"Would that work?" asked Aunt Vivian.

"I don't know. But it's worth a try," replied Aunt Lena.

"Mind letting everyone else in on what is worth a try?" I said.

"Mallis took a sample of your blood, Allie," said Aunt Lena excitedly. "That was how his witch was able to attack her in both the astral plane and the physical one. There is a lot of power in one's blood, after all. Likewise, there is a lot that someone who is practiced in the arts can do to another with their own blood."

Aunt Vivian was nodding as she sat next to her sister.

"But there is a difference, sister. Our unknown witch had a sample of live blood to work with. Blood magic is contingent upon the condition of the subject's blood. In this case, Elion did not save a sample of the creature's blood the way Mallis did with Allie. Plus, he technically isn't alive; his heart doesn't beat…who knows what effect he would have on another supernatural even if he were to have saved a true sample the blood?"

"That's true," acknowledged Aunt Lena, "but you're forgetting one thing. He also has a bit of Allie's blood in his system. Her magic could provide the spark we need to 'read' the hound's blood and get a hit on it. Plus, the very fact that Elion has no circulatory system could play in our favor. A vampire absorbs the blood of its victims, but not in the same way that a human absorbs nutrients. How long does the blood stay in your system?"

Elion shrugged. "It depends on the level of activity following a…meal. And the age of the vampire. The older the vampire, the longer it remains in our system, because we don't need as much blood to sustain us anymore."

"So there is a possibility that the blood of the hellhound could still be in you, right?" The vampire nodded in response.

"So we try to work some blood magic of our own," said Aunt Lena. "Or, more precisely, some blood *memory* magic."

"What will that get us?" I asked. Cody had moved closer now, curious about what my aunts were planning.

"Well, if we do this the right way, and we can tap into the hound's blood, we should be able to use the hound as a lens…a way of knowing what it knows," said Aunt Lena.

"Kind of like using it as a living scrying crystal," I said.

"Yes! Exactly," said Aunt Vivian. "If we are careful, we should be able to divine our enemy's location."

"Assuming that the hound went home, of course," said Nate.

"He would have," said Rob, speaking up for the first time. "A wounded animal will return to its master. It will respond to its instincts."

"It would have," said Elion. "Mallis pulled that thing from a dark dimension. And in so doing, he would have put it under his yolk, just like the wolves he commands. The creature would have followed the rest of its new pack back to Mallis."

This was good. It might just be the break that we needed. "How do we go about doing this?"

"This particular type of magic falls under your aunt's purview," said Aunt Vivian eying her sister. "I'll get the supplies." With that, she left the basement and headed up the stairs, no doubt to their shared study.

"Do you need help?" I asked.

"Not with this...but while I am casting this spell I need you to focus on the wards around the house. This type of magic can attract a lot of unwanted eyes. You focus on keeping us veiled, got it?" I nodded and mentally reached out to touch the wards, just to make sure they were all still up and in place.

Elion was pacing the length of the short entryway like a caged panther. I asked Cody if he would mind making a sandwich run. He took Nate and Rob with him, seeming to catch the vibe that the fewer people present for this spell, the better.

"You okay?" I asked Elion.

"Why did you do that?" he asked, standing in place long enough to stare me down.

"What? You mean save your life?"

"My life was not yours to save."

"What are you going on about? Wait...did you *want* to die out there?"

He hesitated before replying and that gave me my answer.

"Allie, I've been alive for a very long time. Longer than you can comprehend. And during that time I've done things—things that I am ashamed of, things that would make you hate me. If you knew...you would not have hesitated to let me die in there." His black eyes were cast downward and I searched the tone of his words to see if there was meaning deeper than what he was stating.

"Maybe you're right. I don't know what you did in your past, but you came to us offering help. Saying that you were reformed, that you were more than your vampiric nature. Was that all a lie?"

His black eyes smoldered as they bore into me. "No. That was all true." He took a deep breath and released a heavy sigh. "I'm tired, Allie. Tired of so much fighting and bloodshed. Tired of literally killing other living creatures so that I can live. You have no idea how heavy the weight I feel is."

He was wrong. I was starting to understand just how he felt. But I kept my mouth shut.

"Look, I'm not going to try and convince you of anything," I said. "Honestly, I don't have time to do that. Instead, I'm going to be painfully truthful and selfish. I don't give a damn about your whiny, emo feelings right now. We are all about to be wiped off the face of the earth, or eaten by ghouls, or who knows...so forgive me if I don't have it in me to indulge your self-pity right now. The truth is, I need you. You're a weapon for me to point at Mallis and his crew. That's what I need from you. Your power, your strength, and your knowledge of the enemy. I don't give two shits about what you do after we win this fight. And mark my words, we will win. Failure is not an option." I stepped closer to him. He was taller than me, but I looked up directly into his eyes without blinking. "So hear me, and hear me well. You're going to table your shit, help us defeat Mallis and the Warlock, and then and only then, you can do whatever the hell you want to do with your...un-life."

He didn't say a word, just kept those black eyes trained on me.

"Besides, I think that's all bullshit anyway. If you wanted to die, you could walk out into the sun at any time. But I saw all the carcasses you tried feeding on back there in that hole. You were fighting for your life...there was nothing defeatist in the Elion I saw back there."

There was a ruffle behind us, near the stairs. I walked down the hallway in time to see Hope scurrying quietly back up the stairs, brushing past Aunt Vivian as she returned with an armload of jars filled with various powders and dried herbs.

"What did I miss?" she said taking the temperature of the room.

Aunt Lena, who had been sitting on the couch with her eyes closed during our exchange just shrugged. "These kids and their manufactured drama." She smiled and reached out to take some of the jars from her sister and arrange them on the coffee table before her. Then she motioned for Elion to sit down beside her.

"Allie, mind the wards," she said. "And you, vampire. I'm going to access the memories of someone buried deep within you at this time. This might hurt a bit."

Chapter Sixteen

As I watched Aunt Lena work with Elion, I couldn't help but wonder how much more there was to the art of witchcraft that I needed to learn. Would I ever know everything that my aunts knew? They had a lifetime of practice behind them, while I was so new to my power. Still, I was the Reliquary. Mine was a higher calling and a greater responsibility. Part of me resented the fact that I wasn't involved in the conjuring the blood memory spell. It would have been the perfect learning opportunity.

Stop it, Allie. Concentrate on what you need to do. I reached out with my mind and tickled at the wards. Then I poured some extra magic into them. In my mind's eye, I pictured them as reflective mirrors, creating a dome that would completely mask our house from any and all magical signatures. Still, a part of me couldn't resist eavesdropping on Aunt Lena and Elion.

The two of them sat on the floor facing one another, legs folded beneath them. Aunt Lena held a walking staff across her lap. I recognized that staff from the night my aunts had summoned the spirit of the Warlock to question him in their study. The sight of it and the memory of that night made me shiver. Between them, there was a large silver bowl filled with water. Aunt Vivian stood behind Aunt Lena, both hands on a different staff, the heel of which she had planted firmly in front of her.

"What do you need me to do?" Elion asked.

"Not a thing, dear. Just close your eyes and relax. Don't fight the spell when you feel it," replied Aunt Lena. "Hold out your hands, palms up."

Elion did as he was told and Aunt Lena placed her own hands, palms down, on his. Immediately she withdrew her hands, a surprised look on her face.

"What is it?" said Elion.

"Nothing...your mind is...shielded, it seems. A byproduct of being dead, I assume. No matter, just relax. Concentrate on the moment you bit into the hellhound, what it made you feel, what you sensed through the connection. I'll do the rest."

Again they resumed their previous connection, hands touching above the silver bowl of water.

"*Etrion ature imex*," said Aunt Lena softly, "Mother Earth, give me your sight and show me what the blood remembers. *Etrion ature imex...Etrion ature imex*!" When she opened her eyes, they flared white. Elion's body stiffened in response to the incantation, but he kept his eyes closed as he was told.

Aunt Lena leaned forward and stared into the bowl.

"Don't move, Elion," she said. "You're going to feel a little pinch." She lifted one hand and held it over her head, never once taking her eyes off the bowl. Aunt Vivian handed her a small silver dagger no bigger than a letter opener. Still staring into the water, Aunt Lena took the dagger and opened a small cut in Elion's palm. The wound began to close almost instantaneously but not before she was able to dip the tip of the blade in his blood, like a macabre quill into a brackish jar of ink.

"*Etrion fae namare*," she said, "show me the hidden." Then she placed the tip of the knife into the water and stirred slowly.

The water hissed in response and tiny wisps of smoke began to snake upward from the surface, encircling my aunt as she continued to peer into the bowl. Aunt Vivian raised her staff a few inches off the floor and slammed it back down, causing the smoke tendrils to evaporate and retreat back into the bowl. The surface of the water turned a bright, highly reflective red, and slowly, images began to appear. It was like suddenly looking down into a television screen that needed to be cleaned. A bit murky in places, but moving pictures were definitely forming.

Slowly, a scene materialized in the darkened fluid. It started as a hazy outdoor scene, like someone was running through a field, recording on their phone as they went. A house came into view briefly, a large, stately Victorian with an intricate rose garden leading into a high shrub maze. Whoever was filming ran toward the garden and then the camera whooshed upward at a dizzying rate, only to come back down again beyond the maze, at the bottom of a grand concrete stairway that led to an oversized covered front porch.

Another leap and the porch had been gained. Now, we were at the massive double front doors that led into the house. A nudge opened them and the view suddenly morphed to the interior space of a very well-appointed foyer with a large circular mahogany table adorned with a tall white vase with an assortment of grasses and beautiful flowers shooting out of the top. A grand circular stairway flanked the table to either side, flowing gracefully up to a catwalk landing that overlooked the space.

We moved through the entry and under the overlook, heading deeper into the mansion. A quick turn and the view changed to a large drawing room ringed with floor-to-ceiling bookcases. A massive, ornate fireplace dominated the far wall of the room. It was big enough that two large men could have stood comfortably inside. The room was dark—whatever windows there were let no light into the space. The soft flicker of dozens of candles spread throughout the room provided the only source of illumination.

Our view swiveled to the back of the room, where a large desk covered in intricate carvings squated. Behind it, a figure draped in shadows sat. The figure rose and stepped forward into the light, seeming to walk towards us.

Mallis. I felt my heart quicken and a sudden spike of adrenaline shoot through me at the site of him.

"So…you've returned from your hunt, I see." His voice sounded hollow and far away, like he was speaking through a tin can. It was both eerie and disorienting to hear voices float up from the bowl. "I take it you did not find the injured turncoat? You should have finished him when you had the chance."

"Oh, come my love," came another voice, floating into the space. The hollowness of the bowl made it difficult to tell from which direction it emanated. "The vampire was stronger than you led us to believe. He actually managed to hurt a hellhound."

Our view swung around to the library entrance to take in a tall female form standing in the doorway. She wore a long black dress that pooled at her feet, but her face was covered in shadow. She started to step into the room, but abruptly stopped.

"What is it?" said Mallis, his voice instantly taking on an alarmed tone.

"Don't move and don't speak!" said the woman. She reached, stretching one arm in our direction. Palm out, fingers splayed, she let loose a blast of light that nearly blinded all of us that were looking down into the bowl.

"Allie!" screamed Aunt Vivian. "The wards!"

Damnit! Too late, I realized my attention on them had wavered. I was too engrossed in what was playing out in the bowl of water. Reaching out, I probed the wards, breathing a sigh of relief when I realized they were still up...only something was wrong. They were cracked, splintering in places. I immediately poured magic into repairing them, only to feel them begin to break apart even faster. Large chunks seemed to be sliding off quicker than I could repair them.

"Ummm...something is wrong," I said through gritted teeth. "The wards...they are—"

Before I could finish the sentence, another flash of light broke free from the bowl, this time accompanied by a rolling wave of thunder that split the air. The bowl began to hum as Aunt Lena broke her contact with Elion. They dropped their hands and eased away from the glowing basin. Just as quickly as it appeared, the light vanished and the water returned to its normal, reflective state in the vessel.

"Well at least we know—" started Aunt Lena, but her words were cut off as a ghastly hand reached up out of the bowl. The sudden appearance startled both Aunt Lena and Elion as each tumbled back away from the appendage. An arm followed as the hand reached higher out of the bowl, the fingers wriggling and flexing slowly, teasing the air around them.

"Get back!" said Aunt Vivian as she brought her staff forward, aiming it at the arm.

Before she could mutter an attacking spell, however, the fingers straightened menacingly in her direction and again flung a bolt of white light at her, knocking her backwards across the room. Before any of us could respond, the arm wavered, becoming transparent and then disappearing, only to be replaced by black smoke that rose from the bowl, billowing across the ceiling to hang in place, floating in midair opposite myself and Cody. It reminded me of an old show that my aunts used to watch about an misogynistic astronaut who kept a genie enslaved in a bottle and only let her out when he needed something.

Only this puff of smoke didn't solidify into a perky blonde wearing some oversexed male's idea of an Arabian harem outfit. No. This smoke monster slowly became solid, taking on the form of a tall woman dressed head-to-toe in black. I could practically feel her eyes staring at us. At least I imagined they were; I couldn't really tell because a veil covered her face.

"I had hoped it would not come to this," she said, her voice still ephemeral and sounding far away. "But you have left me no choice."

"Witch!" said Aunt Lena. "You have chosen your doom in coming here! And so help me, if you have harmed my sister…"

"You'll what?" replied the witch. "Drown me in tea? Plant me in a garden?"

The menace in her voice drowned out any hint of snark. Time to put an end to this. I raised my hand and conjured a bolt of mystical force and hurled it at the witch. She spun to face me, raising one arm to effortlessly deflect the bolt. The magic ricocheted away from her, shattering one of the sets of French doors that led out to the lower-level deck.

The witch raised the hand she had used to block my magic up to her face, seeming to examine something. "Interesting," she said. She then extended her hand in my direction, unleashing a sizzling blast of magic in my direction. In a blur, Cody was in front of me in hybrid form, taking the brunt of the blast, but it still struck hard enough that it sent the both of us reeling backwards. The impact with the carpeted floor knocked the breath out of me. I landed on top of Cody and rolled over onto all fours, gasping as I tried to see if he was okay. The blast of magic had singed his fur but otherwise had not done too much damage. That was surprising since the blast had been meant for me. Was the witch holding back?

I struggled to my feet just as Cody leapt to his. He shifted to full wolf form and bounded back into the large living space, a full throated growl let her know his intention as he stalked toward the witch.

"No, Cody, stay back." Aunt Lena had risen from her position next to Aunt Vivian. She stepped forward, protecting her sister, staff held before her. "No telling what this one might do with you...stay close to Allie. I'll handle this."

"Handle me?" said the witch. "Are you mad, woman...?"

Her words were strangled off by an unseen force that grabbed her from behind. The witch struggled against whatever held her in an invisible vice-like grip. I looked at Aunt Lena and could see her lips moving quickly as she invoked a silent binding spell. Her staff was aimed squarely at the witch in her grasp, and the end of it made small circular motions in the air.

The witch was lifted off the floor a few feet as Aunt Lena applied more pressure against her. Her arms were held down at her side and her hands bound by magic as she attempted to raise them in my aunt's direction. I closed my eyes and drew upon my magic, willing my senses to see the unseen.

When I opened my eyes I could see the wispy mystic chains that Aunt Lena had conjured to hold the witch in place. But I could also see the raw power the witch was drawing on to combat her bindings. I could see the strain in the chains as Aunt Lena struggled to maintain them; they weren't going to hold much longer.

I moved to the center of the room and gestured at the witch. I called upon my own version of bindings and reinforced the chains that were thrown around her. Instantly, I could feel the witch's strength. She called upon blackness and asked it to help her break the spell that bound her. I could feel the dark come creeping into the room. It seeped in from all directions, snaking across the floor to do its master's bidding.

I could feel the dark tendrils crawl around me as they sought a way through my defenses. They crept stealthily up behind Aunt Lena, pillars of evil that were erected behind her, waiting to topple forward and crush her under their relentless weight. My warning scream was cut off as one of the black wraiths clawed at my throat, attempting to choke the life out of me.

I dropped the spell I was using to help bind the witch and instead focused on keeping the blackness from worming its way into my mouth and lungs. The sensation caused me to flash back to first attack the witch had launched on me when I was on the deck, and I could feel my adrenaline rush giving way to crushing fear.

"Allie...!" came a deep voice, cutting through the terror. The blackness was smothering now, engulfing me and threatening to carry me away. "Allie!" It was Cody's wolf calling to me again, threatening...hungry.

"Allie, snap out of it! Do something!" No. Not the wolf. Just Cody...he was imploring me...pleading for my help. "She's going to kill Lena!"

His words cut through the darkness and struck me like a red-hot knife.

No. This was not about to happen on my watch. "*Evultis!*" I shouted a single word meant to expel darkness and let in light. Blue fire erupted from inside me, flaring out in all directions. It burned through the blackness that sought to bound me. The flames hugged my body, suffusing me with warmth and safety. I could feel myself floating in the air, held aloft by the power of my determination and will.

Power flowed from my eyes as I regarded the scene before me. The witch had broken free of the binding spell Aunt Lena had thrown around her. She was advancing on my aunt with what looked like a mystically manifested black blade that glowed and spit dark magic. She held her free hand out before her, hooked into an obscene claw position. Aunt Lena had dropped her staff and was grabbing at her throat with both hands, trying in vain to free herself of the invisible force that was choking her.

"No," I said calmly, reaching out with my magic to snap the force that was strangling my aunt.

The witch hissed at me, spinning around to send her dark knife flying in my direction. But my power was a song within me. It flowed through every fiber of my being in a way I had never felt before. Time slowed, and the knife seemed to be flying at me in super slow motion. I looked over at the witch only to see her frozen in space, her knife hand still extended in my direction. I glanced at Aunt Lena and Cody, both of whom were mired in place as well; the only signs of motion were the slight tracking movement in their eyes as they tried to take in the scene around them.

I returned my attention to the knife coming at me. There were a hundred things I could have done to avoid it. Instead I held up one hand and let the knife strike my palm. It burst into a sparkle of black light that drifted harmlessly to the floor. I willed my body to float calmly over to the witch. She was still facing towards where I had been standing. I reached out and grasped her hand in one shoulder and placed my other hand on the veil that shrouded her face.

"Okay, let's see just who you are," I said as I started to remove the covering.

"No!" she screamed, her own power bursting through and breaking mine.

But it was too late. I had a grip on her veil and the eruption of power that flowed out of her cast me back, but the witch's covering came with me. I landed in a crouch, veil in hand and stared at the back of the witch's head.

I could see the shocked look on Aunt Lena's face as she stared at the witch. I readied an orb of power in my hand as she turned to face me. The orb flickered and was extinguished as I felt my heart shatter.

"Mom?" I whispered.

Chapter Seventeen

My magic flickered away to nothing as I dropped to the floor. My knees buckled and I crumpled like a puppet with cut strings.

Aunt Lena's face went hard as she looked at my mother. "How...how is this happening?"

My mother stepped back, smiling as she regarded us. "'How' isn't important, sister. What is important is that you know that tomorrow is the Leveling. And it will mark the end of your days."

Then she raised her arms from her sides and slammed her hands together. There was a blinding flash of light accompanied by an enormous clap of thunder that rocked the house. When my vision cleared, she was gone.

I was in shock and couldn't find my words. My limbs felt like lead as I sat there, numb to my surroundings.

"Allie, was that...?" Cody asked.

All I could do was nod, throwing my aunt a questioning look. She nodded in return. Aunt Vivian was starting to stir and reached a hand up for her sister to help her to her feet.

There were tears in her eyes. Clearly, she had seen the same thing we all had.

"I don't understand..." I started to say before I was cut off by Aunt Lena. She had her staff in hand and abruptly swung it in Elion's direction. The tip of the staff glowed white-hot with mystic fire and Aunt Lena held it inches from the vampire's face. Elion raised both hands to show that he meant no harm, turning his face from the fire.

"Okay, enough games, vampire," Aunt Lena said coldly. "You tell me what you're hiding, or I swear I will give you a burn that will make what the hellhound did to you look like a baseline tan. What are you hiding from us?"

"Aunt Lena, what are you doing?" I asked, stepping forward.

"Stay out of this, Allie," she replied, never once taking her hard gaze off Elion. "I may not be able to kill him, but I'm betting I can hurt him really, really badly." She inched the staff slightly closer to his face. "What were you hiding from me when I was in your head? Why were they so shocked that you were able to survive the hellhound? From what I saw, even you should not have been able to survive that. Who was that creature actually summoned for?"

Elion turned his face until he was looking right at my aunt, his nose nearly in the glow of her magical fire. I could see the skin on his face deepen in color in response to the heat.

"Me," he said. "The hellhound was summoned for me."

"Why would they send a hellhound after you?" Aunt Lena asked. "I swear, if you have been playing us all this time..."

"I have not been playing you. I swear that is the truth. Everything I have said has been the truth."

"Why would Mallis go to that kind of trouble to kill

you?" she asked. "You said that the hellhound was summoned to augment his army and to destroy us and the shifters. If that isn't the truth, then you have been lying to us."

"No, the monster was summoned to kill me. But Mallis also planned to use it against her as well." He jerked his head in my direction.

I stepped forward, giving him a long look. "The night we met, you said you had been attacked by Mallis's wolves. Was that true?"

"It was. Mallis had just summoned his hound. He turned it on me, but the hound was too weak and disoriented from its cross-dimensional travel to summon its full strength against me. The wolves attacked as well, adding their power to that of the hound. I escaped and traveled here, knowing that the wolves could not cross your wards. At least I hoped they couldn't. Everything else has been the absolute truth."

"The enemy of my enemy is my friend," I said softly. He nodded in agreement. "What did you do that made him want to kill you? It had to be more than just disagreeing with his plans."

He was silent and I could see his temples pulsing, almost as if he was fighting with himself as to how to answer that question. I motioned for Aunt Lena to extinguish her flame and lower her staff.

"Elion, I just saw my dead mother try to kill us. If there is anything you aren't telling us, now is the time. Because something tells me things are about to get dark...in the literal sense of the word. So if you're holding back, then you aren't with us. And if you aren't with us..." I let that dangle in the air, my meaning crystal clear.

"I knew what Mallis had been planning for some time. I

thought it was just another one of his mad schemes. I didn't really think it could be done...at least not by him. This was when he only had the services of the Warlock, and no matter how many witches the Warlock drained, I knew that he would not have the power to cast a spell of the magnitude that would be required for the Leveling.

"Mallis knew it as well after a while. That was why he came up with the plan to bring back the witch that held the Warlock imprisoned in the caves. He knew a witch that powerful...one that was tied directly to the power of the ley lines could certainly accomplish his needs. I thought that was folly as well. The witch had been destroyed...or so the Warlock had told Mallis.

"But she wasn't. She was simply lost...in a kind of limbo. Mallis was able to craft a spell, powered by the Warlock's stolen magic, that could call the witch back to this realm. It was the blackest of magics that did that; and the darkness of the act also bound the witch to Mallis, much like his wolves." He turned to face me again. "I swear, I had no idea she was your mother. When I found out what he had done, what he planned to do, I told him I would not allow it. I tried to kill the witch."

My heart was trip-hammering at his words. "Why wouldn't you tell us this in the beginning?"

"What? Why wouldn't I tell a family of witches that I intended to kill one of their own kind? Even though I had no idea who she was, I didn't know how you would react to that. You were already suspicious that I might be working for Mallis. Had I told you I was an attempted witch murderer..." Now it was his turn to leave something dangling.

"What else?" said Aunt Lena. "Why would Mallis summon a hellhound to kill you? Why didn't he just do it himself?"

"Because he can't," said Elion. "Mallis is my brother. My younger brother. I was turned before him, and I was the one who made him."

The silence was broken by a voice from the stairwell.

"What kind of fucked up family reunion is going on around here?" said Hope, entering the room for the first time. She looked at me, shaking her head. "Your mother, his brother...it's like a messed up daytime soap...*Days of Our Undead Lives*, or something."

"Hope, are you okay?" I asked. In all the commotion I had forgotten she was in the house.

"Yeah, I'm good. At the first sight of all that fighting I hid in the closet upstairs until it got quiet. Then I crept down here to hear all the family drama going on." She walked over and placed a hand on my arm. "Are you alright? Was that really her?"

I rubbed Hope's hand, grateful for the support. "It was."

"Wow. So what does this mean?"

"It doesn't mean anything," I said, setting my resolve. "We still have a fight to win."

No one said anything. Aunt Vivian walked over to me. "Allie. This changes things..."

"How?" I asked in exasperation. "If Mallis succeeds in what he plans to do tomorrow, then we all die. Not just us... humanity dies." I plopped down on the couch, eyes closed, pinching at the bridge of my nose. "That...that *thing* was not my mother. What I met in the cave, that was my mother. This was some kind of bastardization."

I could feel my aunts looking at one another silently.

"You know I'm right," I said without looking up. "Tell me that was my mother...your sister."

Their silence gave me the only answer I needed.

"Whatever that was that just attacked us, there was no trace of her in it. There was only darkness…and hatred. It was a force of pure evil wearing my mother's face; nothing more."

"It will still make it hard to do what needs to be done…" said Aunt Vivian.

"No," I replied. "That bastard has gone too far this time. It will make killing him all the easier." I looked up at Elion. "Are you with us? Because brother or not, I am going to melt that monster."

"I am with you," he said. "What my brother is planning to do will warp the natural order of things indefinitely. It will unleash a hell that he has not yet foreseen, so yes; I am with you."

"What the hell happened here?" Nate was entering the room. He and Rob had a couple of bags of sandwiches that they slowly sat down on the table as they surveyed the damage to the basement.

"Like I said," answered Hope, "fucked up family reunions."

"Long story but I'll fill you in later," I said. "But right now we need to mobilize."

"What are you thinking?" asked Cody.

"Do you know where they are?" I asked Elion.

"I think so. That mansion looked familiar. My brother's MO is to purchase several of them in an area that he moves into and rotate between them. Despite everything, he is still very paranoid. But that one is one of his favorites; it is just outside the city limits, on the way to the cave where…" He didn't have to finish that sentence.

"Is that where they will perform the ritual for the Leveling?" I asked.

"I don't know. Magic is not really my forte. But I do

know that in order to perform a spell of that size they need to be at a nexus of incredible mystical energy to direct it."

"Makes sense," I said. "The ley lines running through this town come together at the caves near Singing Falls. It's probably the most powerful convergence of mystical energy in the Western Hemisphere."

"What are you thinking?" Cody said.

"I'm thinking, why wait until tomorrow to end this? I'm thinking we gather all of our forces and go take that monster out. Or…" I trailed off as an idea started forming in the back of my mind. A crazy, impossible idea…

"What? What craziness has gotten into you?" asked Aunt Vivian.

"Something that just might save us all…or kill us instantly," I replied. "First, we need to get the word out to the shifters and the Totems. We will also need to reach out to Esmee and Detective Walker. Get everyone together. Ready or not, they are moving on that mansion tonight."

"And you?" Cody said. "You said 'they' are moving on the mansion. What will you be doing?"

I gathered them around and started telling them the bare bones of my planes. It was crazy alright, but maybe, just maybe, it was crazy enough to work.

Chapter Eighteen

The warmth of my bed tried its damnedest to keep me enclosed in comfort and safety. I lay with my head resting on Cody's strong chest, one hand absently playing with the light cover of hair that ran down his abdomen.

"You know how I feel about this plan, Allie," he said, moving one arm down to caress me and draw me in closer.

Yes. He had made his feeling perfectly clear earlier. "I know, Cody. But it's the only way. Besides, if it works, it will save a lot of bloodshed."

He started to speak but held his tongue instead. I knew he was only trying to protect me, like always, but now wasn't the time. What we were facing, what I had asked my friends to do, was near impossible. Elion had told us that if Mallis was able to do what he intended, it would be open season on mankind for creatures from the dark realm. They would would make the hellhound look like Snoopy.

The imbalance of magic would spread like a virus around the globe, opening portal after portal to allow all kind of demons and hungry monsters to pour into our plane of existence. There was a reason that things go *bump* in the night; they fear the light of day. Without that fear to hold them back...we as a species were about to get bumped to the bottom of the evolutionary ladder.

"You sure you're up for this? If we play this out the way you plan, she will probably show up."

"I'm counting on it," I said. My mother, or whatever the hell Mallis had summoned up from the abyss, was a wild card only in that the power she wielded was clearly head and shoulders above what myself and my aunts possessed. "Cody, I need you to promise me that you'll stay with the Totem Shifters tonight."

His body stiffened against me in response. "I'm not leaving your side, Allie. So you can forget that."

I turned over on my stomach, placing my chin on his chest so that we could be eye-to-eye. "They are going to need your experience. They will naturally look to you as a leader. And I can't have you with me tonight because I can't risk any distractions. If I'm worried about you, I can't focus on what needs to be done."

"You'll be unprotected. I won't gamble that I could lose you."

"No. I won't be. I will have Nate and Elion with me." Silence in bed is never a good thing. I nudged him slightly. "You know it makes sense."

He sighed and I could hear him swallow hard. "Nate is a saber-tooth. He is a hell of a lot stronger than me, so yeah, I understand it from a tactical perspective. But it still stings a little. You're my girlfriend. I should be the one protecting you."

"It's not about protection. It's about what gives us the best chance at winning. Having Elion there means that Mallis will probably send the hellhound there; and that means it won't be at the mansion where the shifters will be focused. Together, Elion and Nate have the best chance at stopping that thing."

"And where you go, so goes the witch." I nodded in silent agreement. "But what about Mallis himself?"

"My bet is he will follow his witch. He needs to protect his strongest asset. Plus, if he has a blood vendetta against his brother, my bet is he won't be able to resist seeing Elion killed in person."

"There are a lot of moving pieces and bets to fall into place to make this work," said Cody.

"Yes. But right now I really think this is the best chance we have."

"And you're confident you can do this?"

"I have no idea. My power has been growing. But this... we'll see."

I moved up and planted a kiss on his lips. My hand traveled across his hard abdomen and found its way lower, cupping hard warmth. "Well, that was fast."

"Don't you know wolves are known for their stamina and recuperative abilities?" he whispered into my face before nuzzling up against me and easily lifting my body until I rested on top of him. I placed one hand on his chest, my fingers splayed through the light smattering of hair there, while with the other I reached down between us to guide him into place.

Our lovemaking was not tender. It was raw and animalistic in a desperate attempt to possess one another. It felt like our bodies were parched and this might be the last drink of water we would ever get.

We made our way from my bedroom to the large living area just as Elion was coming up from the stairs, followed by Hope. I gave her a questioning look but she refused to meet my eyes.

"Nice jacket," she said, breezing by.

"Hey, it's a motorcycle jacket and will help protect my arms against bite and claw. I hope." Even though it was autumn, it was still North Carolina, so that meant sticky warm days and sticky, slightly less warm nights. This jacket would make me sweat my ass off, but if it saved me from some potential permanent scars, so be it.

Nate, Elion, and Rob all stood opposite Cody and myself, waiting for instructions.

"Okay, so everyone knows what the game plan is, right? Cody will lead the shifters to—" A knock at the door interrupted me, and I turned as Hope walked over to see who was there.

"Sorry we are late," said Detective Walker as she entered the room. Behind her trailed Esmee. "It took some doing to accomplish what you asked."

"But you were able to, right?" I asked.

She nodded. "Singing Falls is now closed in a twenty mile radius surrounding the park," she said. "A methane leak is nothing to play around with." She smiled and winked at me.

"Good. That will minimize the potential collateral damage to civilians."

"You know I may not have a job to go back to after this," added Detective Walker. "If brass finds out it was a hoax…"

"If Mallis turns out the lights tomorrow, you won't have to worry about not having a job," I said dryly. "Did you manage to get the second part of my wishlist?"

"Sure did. All the C-4 I could get my hands on from my military contacts is in the back of my Humvee."

"And you know how to…make it go boom?"

She laughed at that. "You mean detonate it? Yes, I spent five years out of college working demolition for a construction company before going into law enforcement. Didn't use C-4, but how much harder can it be?"

I wasn't quite sure how to take that, but wasn't going to belabor the point with her. "So let's run through this. Nate, Elion, and Detective Walker will be with me at Singing Falls. Cody and Rob will go with Kendra and the rest of the shifter clans to the mansion. Mallis won't be expecting a head-on attack because he thinks we don't know where he is. It will take him a while to realize that I'm not with you. At that moment, he will use his witch to locate us and have to split his forces to try and take us all on. I'm betting he sends a small contingent of wolves along with the hellhound after me…"

"Wait, why would it be small? Why not send them all after you if you're the one he is most worried about?" said Hope.

"Hellhound," I replied. "You haven't seen that thing in action. I'm betting he won't think he needs much more than that to handle me. Plus, my moth—I mean, the witch, will be with them as well. Those are his heavy hitters. But he won't risk coming to the Falls just yet, not until the spell is cast. He won't risk getting caught out in the daylight. So that means he will still need a large pack at the mansion to protect him.

"The eclipse starts at 6:47, same time as sunrise. It will be the first time in five hundred years that this will happen. We will be at the Falls shortly after the shifters launch their attack on the mansion. That gives you"—I turned to face

Cody—"a couple of hours before dawn to take out the wolves. If we prevent the Leveling, it will leave Mallis trapped and defenseless once the sun comes up." Of course that was all dependent upon me being able to hold up my end of the bargain and stopping the Leveling spell from being cast in the first place.

"So, are we sure this will work from your end?" Detective Walker said. I assumed Esmee had filled her in on the entire plan.

"It has to," came Aunt Vivian's voice from above us. She walked down the stairs with Aunt Lena following closely behind her. Each carried her staff in a firm grip. "That's why we are going with Allie as well."

"That wasn't part of the plan," I said. "I can't risk that."

"You don't have a choice," said Aunt Lena sternly. "I know you may not want to acknowledge it, but that thing out there is wearing the face of our sister…and your mother. It will be more than enough to get under your skin; it would get to anyone, Allie. Besides, what you are going to attempt to do will take all of your concentration, leaving you vulnerable to attack. Let Nate and Elion handle the hound, but we will have to protect you from the witch's magics."

"She has a point," said Elion. "I may be strong, but I'm not immune to magic…and neither are Totem Shifters, I would imagine."

"Besides, if everything falls into place, you may be finished with your work before the witch even shows up," said Aunt Vivian. "But just in case, we will be there as your magical backup."

"Alright then." I gave in, knowing there was no point in arguing. "Let's get moving, we all have a lot of ground to cover tonight."

As we all made our way from the house and headed for the cars, I couldn't help but notice how bright and clear the sky was. The stars shone brilliantly against the cloudless sky and full moon washed the landscape with pale blue light.

I gave Cody one last bear hug and a passionate kiss.

"I'll see you soon," he said without a trace of doubt in his voice. I nodded and watched him pile into the Jeep with Rob as they headed off into the distance.

The rest of climbed into the spacious Humvee with Detective Walker, eased out of the drive, and headed for the Singing Falls National Park. I turned my head and took one last look at the house I had called home as it faded into the distance.

Breathing a silent prayer, I beseeched any deity that would listen to please not let this be the last time I would see it.

Chapter Nineteen

After leaving the car farther back from the park entrance than usual, we made the five mile hike to the Falls in near silence. My aunts cast a wide notification net around us; anything with a supernatural signature would immediately set off alarms that only they and I would be able to hear. I had to give my aunts credit; it was a hard hike and they kept up without complaint. I guess being raised in the mountains had its benefits. The look they had given Nate when he offered to shift and carry them was priceless.

We reached the small encampment at the base of the Falls and gathered around the natural pool where the runoff was collected. I looked at my watch and tried not to think of my friends and what was potentially happening to them. At this point, they would have definitely engaged with Mallis. The thought of my friends fighting for their lives without me pulled at my heartstrings. I banished the thought, fully aware of what a distraction could mean for what I was about to attempt.

"How long do we have?" asked Nate.

Glancing at my watch, I realized that sunrise was only about an hour and a half away. The witch would be here just before dawn to begin casting the spell. I held onto the slight hope that Cody would be able to delay them; any extra time he could buy us would be needed. I also knew that the witch and Mallis would cut and run no matter what was going on at the mansion to get here for the ritual. All I could hope was that they would not have a contingent of wolves with them as well. After all, a witch, a vampire and a hellhound would be more than enough for us to tackle. I almost laughed at that thought; it sounded like the beginning of a bad joke…if they were all walking into a bar instead of coming to kill us.

We went about setting up in silence. I reached out with a probing spell, looking for the right place to cast my own magic. I could feel the hum of the ley lines coming from the caves. There was so much ambient power in this area; it hurt me to think about what I was about to do.

"Uh, you sure it's safe in there?" asked Detective Walker. She was looking at the main entrance to one of the caves not far from us. It was dark and foreboding, and in the eerie light of the moon it looked all the more like an open mouth, waiting to slam shut after any unsuspecting prey walked through.

"Yes, it is perfectly safe," said Elion. "There is nothing alive bigger than a cricket in there. I will go with you to set your charges."

"You sure you want to do this?" she said to me. "Once I detonate, there will be no going back. That entrance, and any others we rig, will be closed off forever."

"I know. But we can't risk anything like this happening again. We can't have more humans, witches or supernatural beings having direct access to the ley lines."

Detective Dana Walker nodded and headed off toward the cave, Elion following close behind carrying a large rucksack filled with explosives. We were cutting it close. I hadn't anticipated the hike up here taking as long as it had.

"Okay," I said turning to my aunts, "our turn. Nate, can you bring over the supplies?"

He hefted the second sack he had been carrying and dropped it at our feet. "What do you need from me?"

"Stand watch," I replied, "for anything out of the ordinary. This will take a lot of my concentration so I'm not sure I'll be aware of everything happening around us in time to act."

He nodded and took a few steps back, turning his back to us as he surveyed the woods around us.

My aunts opened the case, took out a few jars of white powder, and began outlining a circle on the ground where I had indicated. They gave me one last look and I didn't need them to voice their question out loud.

"I wish there was another way," I said. "But we are out of time."

I sat down cross-legged as they continued to draw the circle around me. The powder was a combination of rare earth elements and silver nitrate. It was designed to draw in and trap magical energies, and repel attacks from supernatural beings. I wasn't taking any chances in case a wolf were to slip past my aunts or Nate in the coming battle.

I closed my eyes and drowned out all thoughts and sounds around me as I reached deep into the bedrock beneath our feet and felt for the power that thrummed there.

"*Aravas atone silat,*" I said, calling out to the Power of the Stone. I intoned the incantation again, a prayer to Mother Earth to release her secrets.

I banished all thoughts of guilt over what I would have to do and concentrated on the flow of energy that crisscrossed the space around us. The ley lines were the lifeblood of magic. They carried the mystical energies that had fed Trinity Cove since before man had discovered this world.

And this place, here at the base of Singing Falls, was the where the lines all intersected, flowing out like a wondrous web to all magical creatures great and small.

It was Elion that had given me the idea. He had said that the witch would need to cast her spell from a place of great magical energy. There was no greater concentration of magic anywhere than right here. I could feel it, calling out, singing to me. It was a living, breathing creature…and I was about to kill it.

I was a Reliquary, a witch with unlimited magical abilities, or so I was told. My power had been growing in leaps and bounds lately. The more I used it, the stronger I felt it become. When the witch had attacked us in our own home, I had felt it flare out, freezing time and space around me. I should have used that moment to kill the witch, but my aunts had been right: whatever she was, she was wearing my mother's face, and it had made me pause.

But the feel of my magic at that moment was something I had never dreamed capable of possessing. For a split second, I was one with the ley lines; I could feel the entire world moving through me. I'd felt like I was everywhere and nowhere all at the same time. My consciousness had expanded to the point that I understood what I needed to do. Now, I had to hope that I would be able to pull it off.

I pushed my senses deeper into the earth, grabbing at the energies that dwelled there and pleading for it to rise up and fill me with power. Power that I could use to kill the witch.

But what would that solve? Getting rid of her would end the immediate threat, but there would always be another witch. And another vampire to replace Mallis. And another eclipse. And so on and so on, until finally someone came along with the knowledge to do what they had failed to accomplish.

No. Killing her wasn't going to end the problem. I needed to cut the ley lines off from this world entirely. Turn off the magic at its source.

What that would do to myself, my aunts, and all of the other supernaturals in the world, I had no idea. But if it meant that mankind would never again have to face the threat of an endless night, then so be it.

I pulled in more and more of the power flowing around me until I thought I might explode. I started to think that my aunts might be wrong; maybe there *was* an upper limit to what I could do. I opened my eyes and everything around me glowed white with power. I was no longer seeing just the physical world, but the mystical one that overlaid it. Power was everywhere, and I was a part of it.

I looked around to see my aunts screaming soundlessly at me. Their staffs whirled before them and they pointed towards the cave.

I had no idea how long I had been in a trance state, and it took me a second to realize that something was wrong. I turned my attention towards the cave and immediately was snapped back to reality—the tie I was creating with the ley lines was broken, and the world once again returned to normal. The sudden change was disorienting to my senses, but I understood immediately what I was seeing.

The witch that looked like my mother walked out of the cave holding one hand out in front of her, palm out. She was deflecting the magical attacks of my aunts with alarming ease. In her other hand, she dragged the blood-covered body of Dana Walker behind her. A loud cracking sound broke through the fog around my senses as I saw Elion's body fly out of the cave backwards, arching across the space to land somewhere out of view.

Mallis then walked out of the cave, his fists clenched, eyes narrowed, and fangs glinting in the waning moonlight. The red glow that followed him, along with the low rumble of something incredibly big and heavy walking on rock, heralded the arrival of the hellhound as it stepped free of the mouth of the cave.

"Are you mad, girl?!" screamed the witch. "What you are attempting to do is heresy, and I will not allow it!" She dropped Dana and reached out with both hands, sending a searing wave of black magic in our direction.

The spell hit like a charging rhino and I barely had time enough to throw up a counter-shield to protect myself and my aunts.

"Your friends are dead, Allie!" said Mallis. "They died horrifically, thinking they had a chance against our army. It was over before it even began. Did you think we wouldn't know what you were trying? We sensed what you were up to as soon as you began your spell. My witch transported us here to the cave where we ended your friends' attempt to destroy this landmark! Just as we will now end your attempts to snuff out the magic from this land."

"Allie, forget us!" said Aunt Vivian, raising her staff and pointing it at the witch. "Finish the spell, we will take care of this foul monster." She motioned for her sister and Nate to join her, and the three of them advanced on the witch.

I watched as Nate shifted into a saber-tooth and charged across the field.

Anger flared within me as I realized what Mallis had said.

Your friends are dead.

No. That couldn't be true. Cody. Cody was dead?

My anger turned white-hot as I got to my feet. I reached out with my hand and made a fist, grabbing at the power that had been flowing around me. I stepped forward out of the circle and threw a bolt of pure white light at the vampire. It struck the ground before him like a bolt from the heavens, splitting the earth and sending him and the witch spinning backwards. The hellhound easily leapt to the side, and set his sights on a charging Nate. With an unearthly howl, it leapt into the air, flaming claws aiming for the Totem Shifter.

"Allie, no!" screamed Elion from behind me. He staggered into view, holding his right shoulder with his left hand. "She is lying, Allie! Cody is fine and still fighting! They teleported into the cave behind Dana and I. I could see behind them into the portal; the battle yet rages on at the mansion! Cody, and from what I could see, the others, are still fighting! She's trying to get into your head!"

In that instant, before I could react, the witch appeared in a blur behind Elion. I saw Elion's chest jut forward as the point of the witch's black blade pierced his body, exiting through his breastbone.

"And you know what?" said the witch as she let his body fall listlessly to the ground, "It worked." Her body blurred and then she was standing next to me, whispering in my ear. "I'm in your head. And thank you for doing the heavy lifting that will jumpstart the Leveling. You really are as easily manipulated as Mallis said you would be."

I tried to scream as I felt the black smoke of her power

rush to cover my face. Pain clawed at me as all awareness leave my body and I fell into darkness.

Chapter Twenty

The ride back to consciousness was a bumpy one. I felt like had been dragged across a rocky dune and kicked a few times along the way. Hell, for all I knew that was exactly what had happened.

Awareness fought slowly through the fog that blanketed my mind. The good news was I was in too much pain to be dead. The bad news was I felt like I had been strung up—literally. My arms were stretched over my head, bound to something at the wrists. My ankles were bound as well, my feet not touching the ground. I couldn't tell what I was tied to, but the cool, damp air told me I was still outside.

An involuntary groan escaped my lips as I lifted my head to look around. The first thing I noticed was the pale, pink light that was just starting to creep across the sky. Dawn was coming, and with it the eclipse.

"Ah, I had thought you might sleep through this, but I'm kind of glad you're going to be awake for the beginning of a new era for your kind." It was Mallis. I didn't need to be able to focus my vision to see the gloat that was so obviously radiating from him.

Instead, I concentrated on what had been done to me. I tried to twist my head around to see what I was tied to, but to no avail. Whatever bound me was just out of my range of vision in this position. I pulled as hard as I could with my arms but could not loosen my bindings.

"Struggling won't help you. The rope that holds you in place has been magically reinforced. It is proofed against muscle and spell." This voice came from my right and I immediately recognized it. The Warlock.

"I thought you were dead or something," I said. "You master has a new pet…didn't think you were needed anymore."

"Oh, I still have need," said Mallis. "Maybe you were lead to believe otherwise, but that was by design."

The Warlock had been off our radar, and to be honest, I hadn't given him much thought since the arrival of the witch on the scene. I filed that under the never-make-assumptions-or-believe-lying-witches folder for later. If there *was* a later, that was.

"I have to admit, I am impressed by how quickly you recovered from her suffocation spell," said Mallis. "Your resilience is duly noted."

Good, keep talking, I thought. At least this told me that I hadn't been out too long. That meant maybe there was still time. For something…I just wasn't sure what.

"She fared better than the other two," said the Warlock with a laugh.

Other two? Who were…my aunts! I turned my head to the side to where the Warlock's voice was coming from, and could just make out my two aunts. They were bound in the same way I was to what looked like an upside-down

Y, ankles tied to the two bases and arms bound to the single leg that protruded upward. The Y itself seemed to be some kind of dark rock that stabbed upward through the ground, displacing a large amount of earth and debris.

"Thank you for charging up the ley lines that run beneath us," said the Warlock. "You made it susceptible to the witch's commands. She was able to transform it into the black obsidian that you are bound to." He walked into view, an evil grin crossing his face. "You remember that? The obsidian is what I use to drain and store a witch's power. I am going to drain you and your aunt,s and use your power to augment our own to cast the Leveling."

The wave of fear that I should have felt was replaced by searing anger. I reached for my magic, but it felt far away and unresponsive. Whatever that witch had hit me with, it was still lingering in my system.

"No magic for you," came the witch's voice. "At least, not for awhile. By the time it returns it will be too late for you."

She strolled into view, the hellhound walking at her heel. The reddish glow from the monster cast an eerie light on the witch's form, the flickering flames made it hard to focus on her.

Hatred flared inside me at the site of her. "What have you done with the rest of my friends?"

"By now, I am sure the ones that attacked our home are dead," she replied. "No lie this time... they were hopelessly outnumbered when we left the fight. As for the ones here..." She let her voice trail off.

"Never mind them; did you find him?" said Mallis.

"No. My blade should have killed him, but there is no body. No matter, in his condition he could not have gotten far. Once the spell is cast we will find him and easily put him out of his misery."

Elion. They had to be talking about Elion.

"His strength continues to impress…but my blade struck true. He should be ashes by now," said the witch.

"No matter," replied Mallis. "The Black Sun is moments away. Start the ritual. Combine your powers with that of the bound witches to bring night to this land forever!"

I glanced over at my aunts again. They were still unconscious, their heads hanging limply. At least…I hoped they were only unconscious. The thought of that filled me with rage again. This time the rage carried a little spark with it, a blue flame that I could feel building behind my eyes. Again I reached…and again, nothing.

The witch looked up at the sky and nodded. "Yes, it is time."

We were bound in the clearing, and I could hear the rush of water that flowed from the Falls to the pool somewhere near us. I watched as the witch and the Warlock moved to stand in front of me and my aunts.

The witch raised her hands and face to the heavens.

"*Ethnea ni arturin!*" she exclaimed, her voice rolling across the clearing, loud and strong. "By all that I hold most unclean I command the Earth to hear me and open! *Ethnea arturin! Ethnea arturin!*"

The Warlock joined in her chanting, repeating the same incantation and adding his voice to hers. In response, the ground around us started to heave and roll. Cracks appeared beneath us, racing outward in all directions. Pink light began to glow upward from where the earth was splitting open, and I could feel the buildup of mystical energy charging into the air around us.

No! every instinct I had screamed at me. This was wrong...this was a corruption of the power of the ley lines unlike anything I could have ever imagined. I watched in horror as Mallis strode towards the witch...this time dragging along two bodies behind him. He dropped them unceremoniously at the feet of the still-chanting witch.

One of the forms stirred, and a soft moan escaped its lips. It was Dana, and I felt my heart lurch. She was alive, but just barely. I watched as the Warlock bent down and callously rolled the detective onto her back so that she faced the now-darkening skies. The other body remained crumpled in a heap, but I could tell from the outline it was Nate.

Mallis looked over at me and smiled, his fangs fully extended and gleaming. "Thank you for bringing me my first meal under the Leveling! Honestly, she will only be an appetizer. The main course will be the shifter that was with her. I'm not sure what he is, but he smells incredible."

I tried to block him out, refusing to let my mind's eye project the horror he was predicting. Instead, I closed my eyes and concentrated like never before, sensing the roiling energies around me...I just needed to touch them, try to shape them into anything that would help me. I probed at my aunts, silently praying they would wake up, but to no avail. The magic around me began to grow, changing and darkening as it became infected with the witch's blackness.

"Now!" she screamed at the heavens.

The Warlock turned and focused his attention on me. His eyes turned a ghastly shade of gray as he extended one trembling hand in our direction and began to softly chant to himself. Instantly I felt it: the clawing of his dark magic as it made its way into the very depths of my soul. Every fiber of my being cried out in revulsion as I felt the mystic energy within me began to leach outward.

I looked over at my aunts, and I could actually see the power being drained from them. The black obsidian they were bound to began to pulse, almost like it had its own heartbeat. No. Not a heartbeat of its own, but rather that of my aunts. It was beating in rhythm with their own fading life-forces. I watched in horror as gray tendrils of magic were pulled from them, wafting slowly over to the Warlock.

The bindings holding me tightened slightly as I struggled even more, returning my attention to the witch. She was hovering off the ground now, the magic she was warping holding her aloft. The Warlock turned and raised both arms in her direction. His body glowed as he poured his stolen magical essence into the witch, feeding her, making her stronger.

The earth beneath her opened up, and white light flowed from it to her body, before she was shot upward into the sky in a single ray of devastating power.

My body shuddered inwardly, sickened by the display of black magic that was destroying the natural order of things. I could feel myself weakening…the Warlock was pulling my magic away and using it to feed the spell that would destroy my world.

Wait. Maybe that was not such a bad thing! His spell was tethering me to him, and through him, to the witch. Maybe, if I could just tap into that link…try to control it…

Instead of fighting against the Warlock's spell, I gave into it, letting my power pour forth and flow into the link he was creating. Through him, I could feel the enormous, primal power into which they were tapping. I could feel the witch taking all of the stolen power that was flowing from us and bending it to her will. Her chanting increased as she focused our magic, pushing it deeper into that of the ley lines, degrading their power and drawing them further away from the natural order of things.

The earth around me moaned in response to the violation.

I could sense my aunts' life-forces fading. Their magic was almost gone, and when the last reserves were leeched from their bodies, they would be no more. Panic and anger set in, the kind that I'd felt in our basement when the witch first attacked us.

I could feel more power swell up within me and I used it, reaching out to probe the minds of my friends lying at the Warlock's feet. They were too deep into casting the spell to notice. I probed at Dana's mind but unconsciousness had clamped down on her thoughts, yet still i probed, going deeper until she opened her eyes and looked my way. She nodded and slipped one hand into her pocket, bringing out what looked like a small double AA battery, a single red dot on the end of it. I mouthed the words "do it" to her and closed my eyes as she depressed the button.

The sound of the blast was devastating as the satchel of C-4 detonated inside the cave.

The mountain shook from the explosion, triggering a rockslide that caused the opening of the cave to collapse. It wasn't the controlled detonation that Dana had hoped for; Mallis must have attacked Dana and my friends before they could complete their strategic deployment of the explosives. That was fine. I had wanted to seal off all possible entry points into the cave systems, but now I would just settle for the distraction that the massive blast caused.

I felt the ripple of disturbance in the magic around me, including the slightest interruption in the binding spell that locked me to the obsidian. It wasn't much, but it would have to be enough.

I focused my magic and pushed it into the rock I was bound to, breaking the binding spell. I dropped to the ground. My movement immediately attracted the attention of the Warlock, and he turned and sent a bolt of crackling black magic at me. I deflected the bolt, sending it at the obsidian that bound my aunts, blasting them free. They toppled to the ground and I could see that they were still alive, but were far too weak to help me.

This didn't escape the Warlock's notice. "You're too late to stop the Leveling, Allie. And you can't fight us alone!"

"Well. It's a good thing I'm not alone then," I replied.

Before he could react, the air around us was shattered by the cry of an enormous bird of prey. From above, a shimmering, blue harpy eagle descended rapidly on us. I didn't think I'd ever been happier to see a Totem Shifter in my life.

But I was wrong. Because sitting astride Austin's back was Kendra in her human form. With her high ponytail trailing behind her and silver blade held aloft, she was a magnificent and welcome sight.

They weren't alone. Through the woods I heard another crash, and turned to see more of my friends breaking through the trees into the clearing. They were led by a golden lion and huge, ivory unicorn. Behind them came bear, elk, wolves and various other shifters headed straight for us at a sprint. My heart skipped a beat as I saw the large, dark form of a werewolf bringing up the rear, running full-speed towards me and my aunts.

Cody.

He darted ahead of the others, his wolf form becoming a blur as he raced to my side. As he approached, he leapt, shifting to his hybrid form in mid-air. He had been carrying something in his mouth as he ran, and when he'd shifted he'd dropped it into his hand. As he landed at my side he threw the bloody, severed head of Shira toward the witch, where it landed and rolled to a stop at the feet of Mallis.

The vampire did not even try to hide his rage. "You will all die for that!" he shouted.

It was then that I noticed that the witch had dropped a significant portion of her power and turned her back, raising both arms in the air. Black magic bloomed around her as she opened a portal; a large, smoldering hole that split the air. Through it poured Mallis' army. Wolves and apostles came forth in a wave that rolled towards my friends.

Chapter Twenty-One

The clash of the two armies coming together reverberated throughout Singing Falls.

The witch's concentration may have been broken, but mine wasn't. I gestured into the air, throwing as much magic as I could at the spell she had been casting. Only the witch who cast a spell could call it back or undo it, and as I probed at the spell and then the earth and air around me, I realized it was too late. Even I couldn't reverse what she had begun. The Leveling had been cast and the eclipse had started. Darkness began to fall across the landscape and with it, my hopes at being able to stop this evil.

"Allie!" growled Cody, "The eclipse has started!"

"I'm too late Cody...there is nothing I can do!"

He grabbed me by my arms, forcing me to look at him. "It's never too late, Allie. I have faith in you. You need to stop this!"

Didn't he realize that was all I wanted to do? That it was all I had been thinking of since all of this shit started? But I wasn't strong enough. My last ditch plan had failed and now, our world was going to die as a result.

Wait. Our world. Maybe that was it.

"Cody! I have an idea! But I need a few minutes to make it work. You have to distract them; buy me some time!"

He didn't hesitate. Spinning away from me, he shifted into his full wolf form and sprinted for the Warlock, unleashing a long, powerful howl that served as a rallying call to the rest of the shifters. In the darkness, he disappeared almost immediately.

The sound of battle was everywhere. The screams of the dying mixed with the roars and shrieks of the attackers in a terrifying cacophony of supernatural war. Flashes of magical light illuminated the air as the Apostles fought along with Mallis's wolves. The impact of thunderous blows being traded echoed across the clearing. The horrific sound of bones cracking and limbs being ripped away assailed my ears. But I refused to let any of that deter me. I had one last shot at this, and by God I was going to make it count.

Turning, I located my aunts and ran to their side. A wolf appeared almost instantly and charged at me, jaws open and slobbering. I struck with a full-force blast of blue fire that incinerated the werewolf on the spot, snuffing out its life before it had the chance to howl in pain. I continued running, sprinting through the cloud of ash that seconds before had been a living, breathing, supernatural being to reach my aunts. They were still unconscious and defenseless. I placed both hands on the ground and sent my magic traveling into the stone that the Warlock had used to bind us and drain our magic.

Breathing an incantation of protection, I commanded the obsidian rock to reshape itself, growing further out of the earth so that it curved into a protective dome that settled over my aunts, cutting them off from the life-and-death battle around them. This would hold up to almost anything that stumbled across them, keeping them safe. At least I hoped it would.

A blast of orange light, accompanied by an ear splitting roar that rattled my teeth, caught my attention. I turned to see the hellhound at full flame, blazing feet firmly planted in the ground, head down with what looked like molten lava dripping from its fangs. Its flames illuminated the area around it, and I could make out several shifters circling the beast. Cody and Jhamal, along with Jase in full, splendid unicorn form. They circled the great beast warily, but before anyone could attack another roar split the morning air.

Nate stalked forward, his large saber-tooth body nearly the equal of the hellhound's in sheer size. In his jaws he carried the limp form of a large werewolf which he callously threw aside, and joined in with the others as they closed ranks on the hellhound. The hound roared his defiance and pawed at the earth, scorching the ground with his fire as he readied for the attack.

That was the opening I needed. I summoned my magic, feeling it flow all around me. The disruption to the ley lines meant there was an excess of energy crackling all around me. Tapping into it, I fought my way across the clearing, blasting through wolves and apostles alike until I reached the witch. She stood with her back to me, face to the sky, her lips still moving as she silently invoked more of her black magic.

"That's close enough, my dear," said Mallis to me. He was standing only a few feet from the witch, and even with magic enhancing my eyesight, I had not seen him. His fangs were slick and red with blood. He dropped the body he had been feeding on. "I told you she would be my first under the Leveling. She wasn't as tasty as you, of course, but then again...few are."

I looked down at Dana's body that he'd dumped so carelessly, and it filled me with rage. My fists glowed bright blue as I readied a bolt of magic to fry his smug ass.

"No," came a calm voice from behind us. "Don't waste your power on him; do what you have to. I'll handle Mallis." Elion stepped into the light that was created by the glare of my magic. "I begged you not to do this, brother. You've pushed my hand, and I am sorry for what I have to do."

Before Mallis could respond, Elion was at the vampire's side, one hand clamped around Mallis' throat. He lifted the vampire into the air and slammed him to the ground with enough force to shake the clearing. Mallis fought back, roaring in defiance as he struggled to his feet and struck Elion a blow that nearly doubled him over. He grabbed Elion, wrapping both arms around the smaller vampire in a bear hug, pinning his arms at his side. I watched in horror as Mallis leaned close, fangs extended, targeting Elion's exposed neck.

Elion reared his head back as far as he could before slamming it forward, his forehead smashing into Mallis' face with bone-rattling force. The impact forced Mallis to break his hold on Elion, who then clasped both his fists together and struck Mallis a blow that sent his body tumbling into the air. Instantly, Elion disappeared in the same direction Mallis's body had flown.

Throughout the entire encounter, the witch had not moved, her body still rigid as she continued her chanting.

I raised my hands, already forming the spell in my mind that I hoped would accomplish what I needed. Before I could trigger it, however, I felt a tightness wrap itself around my throat. Black energy passed through me as I instinctively grabbed at the tentacle around my neck that was threatening to choke the life out of me.

The Warlock. Damnit, how had I forgotten about him?

His magic pulled me close, dragging me backwards until I could feel his fetid breath on the back of my neck. "I know that the act of taking your life was promised to another, but I think I will be forgiven just this once," he breathed. A black blade materialized in his hand, the razor-sharp edge glinting in the darkness as he raised it to my throat. "I'll make it fast, I promise."

Before he could make good on his threat, a black shape slammed into both of us, knocking us to the ground. I rolled over onto my stomach, just in time to see a large, catlike creature pounce on top of the rattled Warlock.

Kendra, in full were-panther glory.

"Hold him!" came another voice from close by. In a flash, Esmee leapt at the grappling figures, her silver rapier cleaving the darkness as she stabbed downward repeatedly. I rolled to my feet, ignoring the screams of a dying Warlock, and returned my attention to the witch.

She was facing me this time, an evil grin making a mockery of the face I had once loved.

"It is done," she said. "The sun is gone, little one."

"No," I replied stepping forward. "That's where you're wrong. See, I realized something. You can't erase the sun... it's still there, we just can't see it. The Leveling is nothing more than a *forbidding*...like the one that imprisoned the Warlock for a time. Like the one that separates our world from the dark dimension where you found the hellhound. And probably where the Warlock and Mallis were able to pull you over from. You're not my mother, bitch."

The Return of the Witch

I focused, drawing on the eldritch energies around me, and struck out at the witch. She readied a shield, bringing it up to deflect my bolt. But that was her mistake. It wasn't a blast that was meant to repel her, but rather one that was meant to attract. The power split when it hit her shield, snaking around her and embracing her dark form. It pulled her to me, locking us in an intimate embrace.

"My mistake was trying to figure out how to stop you *before* you cast this spell," I said, "and when I failed to do that, I panicked, thinking there was nothing else that could be done." I increased the magic that held the witch, and reached out to place a hand on her forehead.

"What...what are you doing?" she asked, struggling in vain to free herself.

"In order for you to cast the Leveling, you had to bind yourself to the power of the ley lines. It was the only way to corrupt it to such a degree. I'm betting that you're still connected in some way...ah yes, there it is..." I could see the black tendrils of power that entwined the witch to the ley lines, snaking upward into the atmosphere, disrupting the moon's natural progression and somehow locking it in its path across the sun. The amount of power to do this was unfathomable to me. At least it was—until I realized that all she had done was warp a *forbidding* into a cylinder that focused the darkness of the eclipse into one place. All she was doing was preventing the eclipse to progress through to its end, when the sunlight would naturally return as the moon's shadow passed beyond it.

Between them, the witch and the Warlock had created a protective ward that would keep sunlight from reaching us. Wards, while still tricky, were something I had become fairly comfortable with lately.

The witch lashed out again at me, trying to summon her

dark smoke and send it snaking into my throat, clawing at my eyes. But I was ready for her. My power hummed within me, and just like back at the house, she might as well have been moving in slow motion. I brushed the darkness away with a wave of my hand and refocused my power into the witch.

I wasn't trying to fight her. I was trying to join my magic to hers, entwine them, and make her power mine. Just as the Warlock had tried with me, I now did to her, absorbing and using her own magic along with mine. I combined our magic and injected it into the ley lines. If I couldn't stop the spell or reverse it, then I was back to my original plan: destroy the ley lines. Cut off the source of magic in our world once and for all. If I did that, perhaps it would keep anything supernatural from deciding to cross over and enter the world of man.

But then I looked around. My friends that were fighting and dying at my side…did they deserve that? I remembered the looks on the Totem Shifters' faces when they realized my magic was able to help them achieve their dreams; to help them see the physical representation of who they had always felt themselves to be. The joy they felt for the first time in their lives…satisfaction with who they were. Who was I to take that back from them?

And what about Cody? He and Kendra were born shifters. What would happen to them if the magic that allowed them to exist vanished? I sighed as I held the witch in place. Whatever I was going to do, I had to do it quickly. I wasn't sure how long I could hold this level of power.

I closed my eyes and quietened the world around me. The din of war around me fell away, taking with it the indecision that clouded my mind. I knew what I had to do.

Pulling more of the witch's magic into my own, I focused on the Leveling.

"You're right," I said to the witch. "It is done. I can't stop it now." I looked at the struggling form of darkness that wore my mother's likeness. "But it's not too late to modify the existing spell." She fought, of course, but she had expended much of her power in casting the spell. What was left was quickly being drained and used by me.

Power exploded within me as I cast my magic outward, pouring it into the spell that the witch had cast. The layers of my memory peeled back as I remembered the first touch of the *forbidding* as I sought to tear it down in order to save Cody's life. That magic had been foreign to me then, something that I'd wielded like a club to smash my way through any and everything before me.

But that was before I learned to control my magic; to embrace what it meant to be a Reliquary. For this to work, I had to reach deep into the reserves of magic that lay dormant within me; I had to accept who and what I was meant to be.

I felt the physical world slip away from me, and the sounds of battle surrounding me grew quiet. All that remained was the warm light of magic that emanated from the ground, the trees, the rocks, the very air I was breathing. I could feel it suffuse every molecule of my being. I reached out and found the spell that anchored the Leveling. It was malevolent and all-consuming.

And it was everywhere. That was what I needed to change.

I tugged at the spell and felt it move; it hadn't quite taken hold. I knew I couldn't undo it...I also knew that in the time it would take me to force the witch to break the spell, it would be too late: the Leveling would have settled in and become the new normal. Honestly, I wasn't even sure *she* could undo this spell. It was massive in scope. I could feel the magic pouring from the ley lines to feed it; enough time had already passed that we should have started to see a sliver of daylight as the sun began to peek out from behind the moon.

But it wasn't happening. It was still pitch-black. I reached out with both hands, feeling for the source of the Leveling. I could see it in my mind's eye…the black smoke that was creeping through the primal light of the ley lines, suffocating and supplanting them in order to keep the sun's energy at bay.

Well, if I couldn't stop the spell, I would definitely have to settle for modifying it.

I grabbed at the darkness around me and began to pull at it. With every ounce of willpower I possessed, I pulled. No spells, no incantation, no invocation of powers beyond the veil. This was just me grabbing onto an ancient, evil magic and fucking it up by sheer force of will.

The effort took everything I had. It felt like I was dying and being reborn over and over. My head was pounding so hard I thought it was going to explode. I was gritting my teeth to the point I was pretty sure they would crack. But I didn't stop, I didn't give in.

I cast my power outward until I could feel the walls of the Leveling, and then I pulled even harder. I needed to stop the spread, isolate it, give it a new anchor.

Slowly, I felt the world around me start to come back into focus. Opening my eyes, I could barely make out the figures around me. There was a shimmer in the air. It was no longer dark, but it also wasn't light out. It was like the waning hours of dusk…that time at night when the sun has set and the moon is just beginning to creep out. The palest of blue light washed across the landscape.

The air around me *whooshed* and I felt myself drop, falling head over heels. I had no idea how high up I had been; in truth I hadn't even aware I'd been levitating. Someone, or something, caught me in mid air; I could feel the grip of steel-hard talons wrapped gently around my waist and chest. The swirling air currents around me settled as I was placed gently on the ground.

Immediately Cody was at my side.

"What...what happened?" I said.

"You tell me," he replied, gently brushing a strand of my red hair out of my face. "One minute we were fighting that hellhound and all the werewolves, the next you kind of went all Dark Phoenix on us, rose into the air...and then this." He gestured around us and again I noticed the twilight glow that seemed to suffuse the clearing, barely outlining the tree band that encircled us in the distance.

"The hellhound!" I shouted looking around and shaking the fog away from my minds eye.

"It's okay," said Cody, placing a reassuring hand on my shoulder. "Turns out he wasn't quite a match for bunch of Totem Shifters. It was pretty sweet seeing a saber-toothed tiger holding the monster down while a freaking unicorn stabbed it through the heart with its horn!"

"And the werewolves?" I asked.

"Routed," said Elion. The vampire walked up to us. He was battered and torn, his flesh rent and raked over in many places. His mouth was black with blood that dripped from his fangs and ran down his chin. "Without the apostles and the magic of the Warlock or witch, they fell. The ones that didn't scattered to the hills once the light changed...after you did whatever you did."

"And Mallis...?" I asked.

"My brother is..." He looked down at his right hand. His long fingers ended in pointed talons that dripped the same black blood that coated his face. "Well, he won't be bothering us again." His voice grew hard at that point, and I knew not to ask any further questions.

"Allie!" It was Aunt Lena. She and Aunt Vivian ran to my side and threw their arms around me. "Oh, thank God! You're alive."

"Barely," I said, smiling. "I feel like a just ran twelve back-to-back marathons."

Aunt Vivian was standing with her head cocked to one side, her attention focused on something far away. "It's still dark here, but...I can sense the eclipse fading elsewhere. How is that possible? Allie, what did you do?"

Cody helped me to my feet and I struggled to find my balance. That spell had taken a lot out of me. "I did the only thing that I could. The Leveling was too big, too powerful for me to stop. So when I realized I couldn't stop it, I grounded it instead. I locked it in place."

"Do you mean to say...?" began Aunt Vivian, letting her voice trail off as she looked around.

"What?" said Cody. "What's happening?"

"The Leveling is still in effect," I said, "but only for Trinity Cove and the surrounding area. I bound the Leveling to the ley lines. I have no idea how far it would have spread if left alone. I assume it could have potentially swallowed the whole of the Earth, bringing eternal darkness to every corner of the globe. No matter. Now, life will go on. Only Trinity will be veiled in shadows."

"You are a fool, girl!" came a creaky voice. It was the witch, speaking up from where she had fallen at my feet. Or what was left of her. Drained of all of her magic, she barely had enough strength to hold her body together. My guess was that whatever she was, wherever she had come from, she was slowing returning to it. Her body was losing its corporeality. Her limbs were deforming, her features sliding away like a grotesque wax figure placed to close to a flame. "You think you did a good thing?" She tried to laugh, but instead only puffs of black smoke escaped her mouth as she glared at me. "All you have done is open the bridge from my world to this town. Everyone from the dark realm will find their way to Trinity...and what will you do when your little town becomes overrun with monsters that make me and Mallis look like schoolchildren?"

"I will do what I must, what I was born to do. I will protect this town and everyone I love," I answered stepping toward her. "But that will mean nothing to you. Because you will not be returning to the nether-place from which you were summoned." I held up a hand and called forth blue flame. "Not even your spirit will return the darkness. You won't be whispering anything to anyone." I gestured toward her and sent a blue fireball screaming in her direction. It struck her form and ignited, burning hotter than a thousand suns but colder than blackest depths of space. I burned her fading flesh to ash, but along with it her soul as well. It was a dark act I performed...and I should have been appalled at what I did. But then I remembered that she had desecrated my mother's name and face.

And I smiled to myself as the last of her evil visage melted away.

No one said anything as my friends gathered around. Their eyes held many questions, questions that I vowed to answer truthfully when asked. But they also carried with them a look of profound sadness. Austin and Lady stood next to me, tears in their eyes.

"It's over," I said soothingly. "It might not have been the victory I imagined, but it's a win nonetheless." Austin gathered Lady into her arms as her friend cried quietly onto her shoulder. "What is it?" I looked around, trying to take in everyone that surrounded us. There were too many people to count: shifters, Totems, friends, lovers, and family. But that was when I realized not everyone was present. "Who?" I turned to Cody.

He took a deep breath and reached out a hand to take mine. "Dana didn't make it." I felt my heart seize up as I finally let the realization crash over me. Cody gave my hand a little squeeze. "Jace lost his brother as well. A couple of the shifters from the community were also lost in the first battle."

I cried then, harder than I had since the early days of my mother's departure. Cody took me into his strong arms and to his credit, didn't try to console me. He just let me empty myself out, providing me the silent support I needed.

Chapter Twenty-Two

SIX MONTHS LATER

The sweet smell of Aunt Lena's hibiscus tea permeated the house, wafting out the French doors to tickle at our noses. I welcomed the steaming cup that she placed before us on a serving tray. She folded herself down on the couch next to Aunt Vivian, facing Cody and me.

"So," she said, "it would appear that everyone has adjusted to our new normal here in Trinity Cove."

I smiled, looking beyond her at the shadow of the woods behind our house. Even though it was midday, twilight permeated as far as the eye could see. It was still jarring to wake up, go to bed, and do everything in between with no change in the natural light outside. My internal clock had taken a bit to get used to what was happening, but over the past few weeks I had come to appreciate the different kind of beauty that eternal night gave Trinity.

"Well, if by 'everyone' you mean the supernatural community, then yes. The humans...not so much," I said.

Aunt Vivian smiled as well. "And you, Cody? How is the police force handling all of this?"

"Actually, not too bad, all things considered," he said. I snuggled up close to him, his body heat adding to the warmth of the tea as it spread through my system. "The brass has called in some specialized recruits from New Orleans that are a little more familiar with keeping the peace among supernaturals than our force. They are making good additions to the team...well, to the officers that decided to stay in the area, that is."

It wasn't just members of the police department that had decided to pull up stakes and leave town when the sun didn't come back out half a year ago. Most of the business owners that had remained in town during the war with the shifters had now left. Tourism, which was at one point our bread and butter, practically fell off the radar as word spread that Trinity Cove was now a hunting ground for creatures out of most people's nightmares. That wasn't true of course; humans were not on the menu for most of the supernaturals that moved into town. Not that they wouldn't dine on one if they could, but they understood and respected the rules that were in place.

My friends and I had come up with the rules. When I realized that Trinity, or the Land of the Settled Sun, as some creatures had begun calling it, was becoming a hotbed for all manner of shifter, fae, witch, goblin, elfish folk, and everything in between, I knew it would only be a matter of time before someone dropped a match on this powder keg. I spread the word that all were welcome here...provided they respected not only any humans that remained here, but one another as well. No race was allowed to feed off another, murder was a no-no, savagery would not be permitted, and vampires, while tolerated, had to register with the town's police department.

That last one was a sticking point...but it was the

shifters and werewolves that came up with that decree. No one trusted a vampire, especially in a town where the sun never rose. And incredibly, for the most part, there hadn't really been any issues that had come up between all these different races of living in the same geographic location. Word had spread in places that I had never knew existed that Trinity Cove was now a haven for displaced creatures of the night, looking for a community they could belong to.

A family of incredibly rich gnomes had moved to town and taken over the banking infrastructure, offering interest-free loans to many so that they could purchase the houses of the humans that had walked away. Slowly, businesses began to reopen under new ownership. We blossomed as a community—albeit a closed one—where everyone respected everyone else's right to privacy and to be who they were without fear.

The Totem Shifter community grew in number and became a cherished part of the community. One of the byproducts of the Leveling spell was that magic now flowed much easier in Trinity Cove than it had previously. It was incredibly simple to cast a spell that allowed the new Totem Shifters that moved to town to make contact with their Kintype. As long as they were truly Otherkin, and their totem was one of positivity and light, they could shift into their new form at will.

Not everyone decided to stay. There were shifters that still ached to be loners, and they made their way back into the high country, or simply moved away from Trinity Cove. But for the most part, we grew together as a community and created a world all our own, sequestered away from the prying eyes of man.

Of course, there were still the occasional curiosity seekers or stray reporters that would wander into town looking to find a story or confirm the rumors of monsters living like humans. In the days following the eclipse, the town was descended upon by what seemed like every journalist from every paper across the globe. After all, it wasn't everyday that one hears about a city that is covered by eternal darkness. Uncovering the truth of it would mean a Pulitzer for all involved. But after weeks of...well, nothing, interest had slowly waned.

Hiding what had really happened had been close to impossible. Many highly respected scientists who happened to be on the high council of the fae court had tried to explain away the twilight that befell Trinity with a lot of scientific mumbo jumbo about celestial alignments and a shifting of the Earth's alignment, the way that certain polar areas could be in darkness for an entire winter. That sounded good, except that we weren't in a polar region.

In the end, help came from a most unexpected source. A reporter for the National Enquiring Minds weekly wrote a story detailing her wild, passionate night with a werewolf in the wilds outside of Trinity Cove, stating that she could one hundred percent attest to the legitimacy of the rumors that Trinity Cove was bathed in constant moonlight; and she was now pregnant with said werewolf's baby. Needless to say, no self-respecting news outlet wanted to be a part of any coverage that could possibly include such lurid details, and thankfully called their reporters home.

But closer to Trinity Cove, many adjoining towns knew what we had become. And they gave us a wide berth, steering any would-be tourists away from the town and the once-alluring Singing Falls. The hiking trails remained closed after the tales of gas leaks and explosions that had caved in a large part of the mountain. The Falls themselves were considered unreachable by authorities, and stiff financial penalties along with potential jail time dissuaded thrill seekers and climbers from venturing too close to the National Park.

Of course, the now and then reports of strange beasts being sighted in the woods around Trinity Cove were enough to keep most at bay as well.

For the most part, our little town settled down and became a lazy brotherhood of like-minded individuals with the single mindset of "live and let live."

"I like our new town," I said. "It feels homey."

"Agreed," said Aunt Vivian. "But there is the still the question of the vampire..."

I squirmed uncomfortably against Cody. "He's dead, Aunt Vivian. You know that."

"We never saw a body," she replied. "Do you really think he could kill his own brother?"

We all knew who she was talking about. Elion had remained quiet long after the fight had ended, refusing to speak about Mallis. "If he weren't dead, we would know by now. And if he's alive and shows his face around here again, we'll deal with him."

Elion had been allowed to settle in the town, one of the very few vampires that were granted asylum. He had taken up residence in a large, abandoned home in a gated community in one of Trinity's ritzier enclaves. Despite everything, he had become a close friend, one that I had grown to respect. But I never questioned him further after that morning in the clearing. One day, when the time was right, I had a feeling he would open up about what had happened. But until then, he deserved as much privacy as the family of fairies that had moved in next door.

"Yes we will," said Cody, leaning over to give me a quick peck on the cheek. "Oh, hey—we need to get going. We are supposed to meet Esmee and Isla for dinner, plus I told Kendra we'd swing by and help her get her new hot tub up and running before then." He separated himself from me and stood up, taking the tray of now empty tea cups with him as he headed back into the house.

"Where is your brother and his boyfriend?" asked Aunt Lena. "I wanted to introduce them to that nice new family next door. You know, the mother is nearly five hundred years old and doesn't look a day over thirty! She said she would show me an herbal recipe for a face cream that will melt the ages away! I can't wait!" She also hurried off into the house, looking for my brother and Jhamal.

Aunt Vivian looked at me and gave me a wry smile.

"What is it?" I asked.

"Nothing, dear. I just hope you realize that you have done a good thing here."

I smiled in return and nodded. "Humans will eventually move back, you know."

"I know," she said. "And they will be welcome. But I think that the ones who do return will know what they are getting into. Word is spreading, no matter how we try to keep it quiet." She stood up, stretching her arms overhead.

"What about you, Aunt Vivian? What are you going to do?"

"Me? I've heard a rumor that there is a Jinn that has opened a bakery around the corner from our coffee shop. I've always wanted to meet one of them. I think I might just pop over and say hello." With that, she too headed into the house, leaving me alone with my thoughts on the deck, looking out with wonder at the dusky world I had helped create.

This town was no longer what it once was. But it was becoming what it could be: realizing a new potential, one where witches, werewolves and shifters could live in harmony, forging a brand new tomorrow. The thought made me smile as I realized that, with all the pocket communities that now made up our town, all the magnificent creatures that were living and working together here, there would never be a dull moment in Trinity Cove again.

My phone rang and startled me back to reality. I looked at the number flashing on the screen and smiled as I raised it to my ear. "Hello, Hope. What's up?"

"Girl! You are not going to believe it but we have been invited to a party this weekend at Elion's place. He says he knows an elf with some kind of wild ale drink that will make us see heaven! We have to go!"

"I thought you were terrified of vampires?"

"Well…yeah. But Elion is not so bad on the eyes. I mean, for someone that is older than Moses…"

I couldn't help but laugh as I made my way indoors. Like I said: things would never be the same again.

More by M.J. Caan

vinci-books.com/tantrichexes

Starting over isn't just about moving on – it's about rising from the ashes stronger, bolder, and hotter than ever.

Turning forty should've been a milestone – but not like this. My husband, my house, my life – gone. And when I say "gone," I mean burnt to ash, leaving me with nothing but a card scrawled with a single word: *The Enclave*.

Turn the page for a free preview…

Tantric Hexes: Chapter One

There are few things that I cherish more than those scant moments when I wake before my spouse and without the aid of an alarm. Maybe I was dreaming about something. Maybe my body just knew that I needed a few seconds of solitude. The kind of quiet that only comes with rousing out of sleep before the house awakens.

Of course, it didn't help that my arm had fallen asleep and the pins and needles stabbing into my hand was relentless. Just one more reminder that my body wasn't what it once was. Like I needed reminders of that.

I remember when sleep was one of my favorite things to do. High school and college Saturday mornings were meant for lounging in bed. But not now.

I don't know why my mind can't just turn off for eight hours like a normal human being. I keep reading that your REM deep sleep cycles are supposed to get longer and longer throughout the night; but that doesn't seem to happen with me. If anything, my REM loses out to my anxiety that seems to never take a break.

About to fall into a nice, deep, tranquil sleep? No. Did you check and make sure the alarm is on? Finally settle down and let that melatonin tea kick in? No. Are you sure you locked the garage door? I mean, it's not like anyone can get into the garage in order to get into the house, right? Well, there are those tiny windows in the garage that a really skinny crack whore could squeeze through and open the garage for her fellow miscreants looking for anything they can fence for a quick buck.

And then that makes me think did I lock the back fence, because anyone could come out of the woods that line the back of the house and find their way inside. No. I definitely locked the fence. I don't even go out there, so why would it be open?

And then, once I finally start to drift off...my husband's restless legs remind me that I still haven't finished watching *River Dance* on DVD that I found at that one garage sale years ago and picked up for a song.

So, when I opened my eyes three minutes before his alarm was supposed to go off, it's not really like a divine awakening. More like finally time to drag my ass out of bed and go have some of the one thing in my life that never disappoints.

Coffee.

But then, in that early morning stillness, something unexpected happened. My husband rolled over, muttering softly to himself, and laid his arm across my body, his hand lightly caressing my breast.

What was going on? I didn't move, afraid to even breathe for fear of breaking whatever cosmic confluence had come together to make this possible. I reached up, placing my hand on his.

He didn't move, just shifted his weight a little next to me.

It had been so long…dare I hope? I swallowed to clear the lump in my throat as I ever so slowly pushed his hand downward until it slid across my stomach and rested just on top of my pajama bottoms. When he didn't protest, I slowly pushed the tips of his fingers under the elastic, and onto the top of my panties. My breath hitched as he stirred a bit more and I pushed a little bit more.

And that's when that damned alarm of his went off.

"Wake up, Blaine, it's time to be productive."

That was his alarm. Some bitch that whispers that phrase over and over, her voice growing slightly louder with each repetition until he finally shuts her off.

Figures. Just when I thought *we* were finally going to be productive, she has to go and break the magic. Fuck.

The alarm startled Blaine, and he tensed, immediately aware of where his limbs were in relation to me. Dare I hope we could continue? He pulled away, muttering something about being sore, and slowly sat up, throwing his legs over the side of the bed as he rubbed at his face and silenced his phone. Stretching languidly, he tossed a mumbled "good morning" my way, and climbed out of bed, heading for the bathroom.

I sighed. Not sure if it was out of frustration from lack of physical contact or relief that I didn't have to perform. It had been so long; I wasn't sure I even remembered what to do.

I exhaled in frustration, my fingers lingering on the soft cotton of my underwear. I listened, waiting for the sound of the shower before I slid the dresser drawer open for the magic bullet I kept hidden under old Christmas and Valentine's Day cards. I pushed aside the slight bit of worry creeping in because I can't remember if I bought new batteries after my last session.

But then, any amorous feelings I might have had for myself quickly evaporated at the sound of his water hitting the toilet like a racehorse, accompanied by an explosive expulsion of gas.

Rolling my eyes, I threw the covers off in frustration and slipped my feet into my slippers as I made my way to my robe and headed downstairs. There, I'm greeted by the eerie stillness of our kitchen. The bare rays of a rising sun were just filtering in through the large windows as I headed outside to pick up the paper that was just delivered. The paperboy has an eye and perfect aim for getting it in the thorny hedges of the rose garden, and I cursed slightly under my breath as I braved the pin pricks to recover it.

Who even has a paper anymore? We do. Or to be more precise, Blaine does. God forbid he just look the news up on his phone or tablet like everyone else in this century.

I heaved a sigh as I returned to the house and dumped the paper on his chair before turning my attention to the fridge. I removed two eggs, some bacon, and a pitcher of milk. In twenty years of marriage, I had never seen Blaine eat anything for breakfast other than two over easy eggs, bacon that was crisp but not "hard", and milk that was room temperature.

He didn't even like coffee, which I have never been able to understand.

I turned the knob of the stove top and was rewarded with fast-paced clicking, but no ignition from the gas. Damnit. Why was this thing so hard to light sometimes? I had told him repeatedly to get it fixed and he had repeatedly told me he was looking for someone he trusted to come in and take a look at it.

I made a mental note to just do it myself later today. How hard can it be to get a repairman to come in and fix a stove?

In the meantime, I felt my annoyance grow. Unless I was willing to light the gas manually with a match, something that always terrified me, I'd have to wait for Blaine to come down from his shower, and that would mean I would be late with his breakfast.

I rummaged through the junk drawer, pushing aside old delivery menus, tape, batteries, balls of cooking twine, and all manner of instruction booklets for appliances, until I found a long candle lighter. If I was going to stick a lit flame to a gas line, possibly resulting in a face-full of fire, then I was at least going to use something that allowed me to keep a good distance from the source.

Carefully, I turned the knob and stabbed the lighter just below the iron rings. A slight *whoosh* and I was good to go. Wiping the sweat off the palms of my hands, I went about making my husband's breakfast.

The coffee maker began to chug to life as I filled it with water and waited for the most perfect smell known to mankind to start wafting through the kitchen. Pouring myself a cup of black gold, I stared at the bacon, watching for the telltale crinkling of the edges that would let me know exactly when to remove it from the pan.

The eggs were plated, and the milk poured when I removed the meat and plated it. Blaine entered the room right on time, adjusting his well-fitting button-up as he moved to sit at the small, eat-in table. My eyes raked over his form, and again I felt a mixture of appreciation and annoyance.

Appreciation for the fact that three days a week at the gym kept him fit and trim, his tapered form augmented by the designer clothes he wore; and annoyed by the fact that I could go to the gym five days a week and it still did little to keep my love handles at bay or stop my hips from spreading a little more than I would have liked.

He always said he didn't care when he would catch me staring at my side profile in the mirror. But then he also gave me a bullet smoothie maker for my forty-second birthday recently. That thing was still sitting in the pantry, and if I had my way it would never see the light of day. But I had smiled and thanked him, nonetheless. At least he remembered, so there was that.

"Blaine, honey, I know you're working on it, but the lighter on the stove is still not working some of the time. And the knob feels weird when I turn it. Can we please get someone in to fix this? You know how it scares me."

He smiled, giving me one of his tiny chuckles. "Babe, like I've said, there is nothing to be afraid of. Just light it manually until I can get it fixed. Not a big deal."

"Well, if it's like this tomorrow, you're going to have to light it and fix your own breakfast."

He didn't answer as he settled down in front of the table, opened the paper and began going down the front page as he crunched some bacon. He paused looking up at me as I stood there, lips pinched together, staring into my cup of black coffee.

"What's the matter? You okay?" he asked.

No, you walking, dangling piece of testosterone, I'm not okay. I hate it when you laugh off my concerns and tell me how to feel about something. Please stop doing that; oh, and why haven't you wanted to touch me in four months, seven days and eight hours? Cause that's how long it's been since you climbed on top of me and grunted one out.

That's what I wanted to say. Instead, I catch myself

replying, "No. I'm fine. I just really don't like dealing with that stove."

He nodded, scooping up some egg. "Alright. It will be fixed by this weekend. I promise."

Hearing that capped my anger a bit. He might be many things, but he had never once not made good on a promise to me. Now, if only I could get him to promise to eat my—

"Oh, and can you do something for me?" The way his eyes landed on me...did he know what I was thinking? Sweat started to break out along my spine.

"Sure. Name it."

"I got a text message that my car isn't going to be ready today, so I'm going to end up working from home again. Can you give them a call later and see how it's coming along? Let them know I definitely need the repairs completed by midweek?"

I frowned. "Sure. I can do that for you. You know, you can just take my car if you don't want to work from home today. I know how much you would rather be in the office."

"True. But I also would rather just wait on my car."

"It's okay. You can come right out and say that you don't want to drive my old Lincoln. I mean, we both know it's no BMW, right?"

He opened his mouth to respond, but instead just chewed on another bite of bacon. Something in my tone must have told him I wasn't in the mood to hear it.

"But no problem," I continued. I looked down at my coffee and suddenly wasn't in the mood for its bitter goodness. "You know, I forgot I'm supposed to meet Jada and Tamara for coffee this morning."

He stood, having finished his breakfast and flashed me a smile. "Sounds like fun. You girls have a good time." He patted his mouth with the napkin, picked up his paper, and headed towards the stairs that would take him downstairs to the office.

"Have a good day. Love you," I called after him.

"You too," I heard, just before the closing of his office door.

I sighed, fished my phone out of my robe pocket, and texted my two best friends asking if they wanted to meet for coffee. Then made my way to the shower. I was craving sugar and couldn't wait to get my hands on one of the bakery's chocolate croissants. Even though I was looking forward to it, I refused to look at my reflection in the mirror as I padded naked across the room.

"I'll do an extra session on the stair master tomorrow at the gym."

I knew that was a lie.

Tantric Hexes: Chapter Two

Emma's Sweet Tooth Cafe commanded prime real estate on the bustling main street of Harpers Ferry, the cute little coastal town I'd called home for most of my adult life. The picturesque, quaint little town off the North Carolina coast that reminded me of a Hallmark Christmas movie wasn't where I had intended to end up.

Armed with a degree in marketing, I was New York bound, ready to take the world by storm. But then, after college, I decided to attend a wedding of my best friend's sister back in her hometown of Harpers Ferry. "It's just for the long weekend," Jada had said. "I'll introduce you to my family and we get one last three-day binge together before heading off into adulthood."

So, I visited with the intent of being here for three days. Until I met the groom's best man. A rather charming local by the name of Blaine Bennet. One look and I was smitten. Two looks and I knew I wasn't going anywhere.

He was the perfect man. For me at least. Just the right mixture of boyish charm, manly looks, and a voice deep enough to cause a flutter in my stomach and my panties when he whispered to me.

Our chemistry was incendiary as we fed off one another. It was like he unlocked passion and desire in me that I didn't know I possessed. The more sex we had, the more of him I craved. We would go at it for hours, until one of us, usually him, was too exhausted for another round. I had never known anything like it, and neither had he.

We were meant to be together.

So instead of a large Public Relations firm in Manhattan, I went to work for a small, community hospital with seventy-five beds in a tiny town in North Carolina I had never heard of. I worked hard, putting Blaine through law school, and then, as soon as he went to work for his father's firm, I quit my job to stay home and help him throw parties and fundraisers.

Thankfully, neither of us wanted children, so at least I didn't have to contend with that. No, by all accounts, I had the life.

And I did. For the first ten years or so, give or take.

"Harlow! Over here!"

It was Jada, half standing out of her leather chair and waving me over. She and Tamara were seated across from the large picture window that looked out onto the main street sidewalk.

I waved and headed over. There was already a large, black coffee on the table around which the chairs were grouped. They each had a small dessert plate with an exquisite pastry next to their coffee. Beside mine sat one of Emma's fresh baked, chocolate croissants.

Taking my seat, I practically moaned when I saw it.

"See. I told you she would be in the mood for one," said Jada, flashing a brilliant smile at Tamara.

"How did you guess?" I asked, taking my first mouth-watering bite.

"Because you only ask us to meet for coffee when you're having a difficult morning. And since it's been a while for you, I could only assume this one warranted a special treat."

"Or maybe I just wanted to see my two best friends for no other reason than I miss them," I answered.

"And that's just fine with us," said Tamara with a smile. "I hate that we've had to cancel our last two get togethers."

One of those was my fault; I had to drive my neighbor to the doctor's office because of a severe asthmatic attack, and the second time Jada had to cancel due to something…unforeseen…as she put it.

"How is your neighbor?" Tamara asked, coyly sipping at her coffee.

"Oh, she's fine. Turns out she was cleaning out her attic and hadn't realized she had misplaced her inhaler until she needed it." I took a sip as well, casting a sideways glance at Jada.

She twisted her lips to one side and rolled her eyes. "Fine! You can just ask why I cancelled."

Tamara and I sat there staring, until finally Tamara blurted out, "So what happened?"

Jada hit us with a Cheshire cat smile. "Damon had a layover in Nags Beach. So…I had to go…lay over."

I rolled my eyes in laughter, and Tamara tsked while taking a bite of her crumb cake. They were polar opposites of one another; Jada was blunt and open, wearing her profanity like a badge of honor at times, while Tamara was far cooler and more reserved, reveling in pretend shock at some of the things that came out of Jada's mouth.

They were the perfect complement to me. I wished I

had Jada's bravado but could temper it with Tamara's gift of reserve.

"You drove an hour to the next town over just to hook up with an ex?" I said.

Jada laughed, making an exaggeration of running her hands across her taut body. "Girl, when the dick is that good...yes. Yes, I did." She turned to stare at Tamara. "You know, he has a friend. I could certainly set you up if you need a little...something, something."

The blush that crept up our friend's face made Jada howl with laughter.

"I'm just messing with you. I respect you staying out of the dating pool till you're ready." She reached over and gave Tamara's hand a gentle squeeze.

Tamara had gone through a rough divorce just over a year ago, and currently had no interest in dating any man. Whereas Jada was single and proud of the fact that she was interested in every man; for a night or two.

Tamara smiled and ran her hand through her shoulder-length, dirty-blonde hair in an exaggerated motion. "Why thank you for that, Jada. Who knows, maybe you'll settle down and date someone as well. Damon, perhaps?"

Jada laughed, shaking her head. Her afro of natural hair framing her face like an exquisite cloud. "Not a chance. All that man's brains are in his pole. Once he gets me off, I have to tune out half the stupid shit that comes out of his mouth."

We laughed again and I could feel the lingering itch that had crept across my skin this morning start to abate.

"So, Harlow, what's going on with you lately?" asked Tamara.

I drew in a deep breath and slowly released. "It's nothing. Honestly. I just needed to get out of the house." I caught myself looking down and picking at my nails. I knew the two of them were exchanging glances and I couldn't bring myself to look at them.

"Did something happen?" quizzed Tamara. There was no judgement in her voice, no pity. Just a genuine desire to listen and support a friend.

"No…but that's just it. Nothing ever happens anymore. I feel like I'm in the Groundhog Day of marriages. I wake up, he wakes up, mumbles something to me, goes to the bath. I get up, make his breakfast, watch him eat it in silence." I felt kind of guilty saying that. It wasn't how it always happened. There were little moments between us that happened to throw that schedule off, but they weren't what stuck in my mind.

"You're in a routine," said Jada. "I mean, you can mix it up a little. You don't have to wait for him to make a move."

I knew what was coming next and dreaded it.

"When was the last time you guys got busy?" she continued.

From anyone else, that would be an intrusive question. From Jada, it was just a typical Tuesday.

"It's been months," I said, whispering the words.

Jada gasped, throwing the back of her hand to her forehead as she mock swooned. "Bitch! Are you being for real? I'm not even married, and I haven't gone that long since… well, we don't need to go back that far. Girl, we are in our forties; our sexual prime. Don't let the fact that all our inhibitions are gone with the wind go to waste."

"Well, it's not the same when you're married," I blurted out. "After a while, things just naturally cool down. Sex becomes an afterthought…it has no bearing on what two people feel for one another, right?"

Jada pursed her lips. "Who are you trying to convince of that? Us, or you?"

"Sex isn't the only thing important to a marriage, you know," said Tamara.

"Thank you. That is so very true," I said. Hopefully my words sounded more convincing outlaid than they did in my mind.

"No, you're right," replied Jada. "But I'm willing to bet that isn't the only thing on the decline. If you can't talk about your needs in the bedroom, I'm betting you aren't talking about what you need *outside* the bed as well."

I squirmed a little, not really wanting to get into that conversation. But she was right. Communication is key in so many areas of a relationship.

I found myself shaking my head. "True. And when I think back to how easy the communication was between us in the beginning, I wonder where the breakdown happened. When did this awful silence creep into every room in the house with us?"

Tamara picked up her coffee. "My bet is that you can't pinpoint a single cause. Lapses like this start small…so small you might not even recognize them. It's not until you realize that you've grown too accustomed to the silence, that you notice how bad it might be."

A third smile rose across my face. "When did you become so wise?"

"I might be speaking from experience, as you well know. Plus, I watch a lot of old Oprah episodes."

Tamara caught me by surprise with that. It wasn't like we ever had to drag secrets out of her, but she was never the first to volunteer something so deeply personal about herself.

"Well, I watch a lot of *Sex and the City*, and I'm here to

tell you if the two of you don't start opening your mouths for more than just talking, someone else will pop up in the picture. For that matter, how do you know he hasn't already…" added Jada, letting her voice trail off.

I was shaking my head. I knew Blaine. He wasn't a cheater. That was a thought that had never once crossed my mind. Jada must have sensed the strength of my conviction because she didn't push the subject. For which I was very thankful. I didn't need to let something like that start worming its way into my mind.

"I'm sorry," Jada said. "It wasn't my place to say something like that."

"No, that's okay. I just…as weird as it sounds, I know that isn't the issue," I replied.

"Well, whatever it is…and I'm not saying there even is an issue…you do need to bring it up. If you're feeling some kind of way in your marriage, staying silent about it doesn't help."

Tamara's words hit home, and again I couldn't help but think that maybe it was coming from somewhere deeper inside her than she was willing to show.

I raised my hands, exhaling sharply. "Okay, enough waxing maudlin. I promise you both, I am going to have a heart to heart with Blaine this week. It's time for us to both check in on one another and get back to making each other feel like a priority. But for now, I just want a distraction. What else is going on? What's good with you guys?"

Tamara's eyes lit up. "Oh, I know. I found the most amazing air fryer online. It has a dual chamber so you can air fry two different things at once."

Jada arched her eyebrows at our friend. "What? Are you serious? You found something like that and didn't tell us?"

She took out her phone and opened it with the tap of the screen. "What's the name of it and where did you get it?"

Despite the way the morning started, I felt my spirits rising. But then I caught movement out the corner of my eye as several people stood up and crowded around the television mounted in the corner of the cafe. There was a single female reporter onscreen with a banner running beneath proclaiming BREAKING NEWS.

I heard her say "...we have this footage from our SkyCam in the area..." and I felt my heart leap into my throat.

On the screen was shaky arial footage of a house fire. I ignored Tamara and Jada as I stood, drawn to the television.

"Hey, what's going on?" asked Jada as she and Tamara appeared at my side.

A woman standing next to us turned. "A house just exploded in a neighborhood around here. Looks pretty bad."

I stared in horror at the picture of a home engulfed in flames. There were bits of it strewn about the neighboring yard as black smoke billowed from the center of what had been my house.

Tantric Hexes: Chapter Three

There was a coldness in the pit of my stomach that was spreading. Even though they helped me upright as I stared at the conflagration in front of me, every muscle in my body was weak and numb. Everything around me ceased to exist; all I could see was the flames being doused with water and the intense hiss of steam being released into the air.

Voices were all around me; news crews, police, fire and rescue…all clamoring away. Some of it was directed at me, others were barked to more voices circulating somewhere in the vicinity. I stared straight ahead, into the flames, unable to articulate what I was feeling.

At some point, someone had placed a blanket around my shoulders, which was strange considering the flames from what was once my home could be felt a half block away.

When we arrived on the scene, I remembered charging at the fire, screaming for my husband. Strong, yet gentle hands had grabbed at me, keeping me from running into the structure. A fireman had me in his grip and was shouting into my face. He wanted to know where my husband might have been in the house, and I couldn't think.

All I knew was that he was in there and I had to get him out.

They were doing everything they could, he kept saying to my face. Hands pulled at me, and I turned to see Jada drawing me away from the man and pulling me to the side along with Tamara.

"Let them do their job, honey. Blaine is going to be just fine," Tamara said, reaching to take my hand and give it a squeeze.

"Wouldn't he have been brought out by now?" I said quietly. There were paramedics everywhere but no sign of Blaine. A couple of neighbors were complaining of ringing in their ears and as I scanned them, I spotted Shelley Blake, the older lady who lived in the house right beside ours. She was sitting on a stretcher while a member of EMS shined a tiny, pinpoint flashlight in her eyes.

I ran to her side. "Shelley...Miss Blake, did you see what happened? Did you see Blaine?"

The older woman brushed the paramedic's hand aside as she looked up at me, her eyes glassy and confused. "I... don't know. I was in the back, watering my roses, and suddenly there was this terrible boom, and everything shook. It knocked me to the ground it was so loud! And when I looked up...your house...oh my God, your house was just gone. There was just this fireball, and everything was burning. I ran to get away...I'm so sorry, dear. But I didn't see Blaine..."

All I can do is try and ignore the numbness flowing through me and keep staring at the house. I shrug off any attempts by the paramedics wanting to examine me. I wasn't in the house. I wasn't the one who was probably blown to pieces in an explosion or buried under tons of debris.

That was Blaine.

That was what happened to the only man I've ever loved.

Everything felt so small and yet so magnified in those moments. I stood there for what seemed like minutes, hours, days. The police inspector was standing next to me asking me questions about the house, but I barely registered it. Until one thing he said resonated and pushed through the fog clouding my mind.

"...or maybe gas?" he said.

I blinked, shaking myself out of my stupor, and turned to face the man. He was older, graying hair cut neatly, and sincere, green eyes.

"I'm sorry, what did you say?"

He stopped scribbling in a notepad and focused on me. "I said, when you were in the house earlier, did you notice anything that might have smelled different? Notice any smoke, or the smell of gas maybe?"

And just like that, I felt my heart drop into my stomach, and I wanted to scream. Bending over, I dropped my hands to my knees, using every ounce of strength I had to keep from throwing up.

"Oh God, what is it? What's wrong?" asked Jada. She had her hand on my back and was slowly rubbing.

When I finally found my voice, it sounded small and far away. "The gas. We've been having problems with the gas stove and...and...I mean, sometimes, the knob is funny and I have to make sure it's off...cos the pilot doesn't work...and Blaine said he's going to get it fixed at some point...but...oh

God, I don't remember this morning if I made sure the knob was off when I left the house."

The officer, Inspector Gerard as I would later learn, swallowed hard but didn't say anything. He nodded, closed his notepad and moved off to speak with some of the firemen.

"Honey, I know where your head is going...don't go there. No way is this your fault," said Tamara softly.

A new batch of tears started to fall as I stood up. I grabbed a fistful of my hair as I ran my hand across the top of my head. "You guys...what if I just killed my husband? I'm always so careful with that fucking stove...and I've begged him to get it fixed. Begged him...he promised it was going to get fixed this week. He promised."

At this point, one of the firemen who had been giving orders and directing everyone else made his way over to us. He took off his hard helmet, shuffling a bit in place as he cleared his throat. I knew from the way he was having a hard time making eye contact that whatever he was about to say was not something I wanted to hear.

"Ma'am, I am sorry to be the one to inform you that we have not yet been able to locate anyone from inside the house. We do have the blaze under control at this point, and in a few hours, we should be able to go through...what's left of the structure," he said.

I bit on my lower lips as I stared intently at him, praying he knew what I wanted to say without me actually having to say it.

Seems like my prayers were answered as he pursed his lips and exhaled. "At this moment, it doesn't look like there are going to be any survivors. But we will know more once we get inside. I'm sorry." He nodded and placed his hat back on before heading back over to his men.

I couldn't breathe.

Everything in my body gave way and I felt myself falling.

Grab your copy...
vinci-books.com/tantrichexes

About the Author

M.J. Caan is an avid reader and writer of all things science fiction and fantasy. Author of multiple science fiction and paranormal fantasy series, M.J. likes to think that there is still magic out there in the world. Even if it's only between the pages of a great book.

www.ingramcontent.com/pod-product-compliance
Ingram Content Group UK Ltd.
Pitfield, Milton Keynes, MK11 3LW, UK
UKHW040923100426
469759UK00003B/42